GARBAGE COP

robert l. bryan

Published by robert l. bryan, 2023.

GARBAGE COP

First edition. July 21, 2023.

ISBN: 979-8223731498

Written by robert l. bryan.

Table of Contents

For Meghan – Always in my Heart.

INTRODUCTION:

When I was ten years old, I had two heroes – my old man and Nick Palmeri. Nick lived next door to us on 83rd Street in Jackson Heights, and he and the old man were as thick as thieves. They had served together in the Army in the same platoon in Korea and had come home after the war to marry two Queens girls and ended up living in adjoining attached homes in a quiet working-class Queens neighborhood.

My old man had picked himself up from a childhood with an abused mother and an alcoholic father to provide a solid middle class lifestyle for my mother, sister and me. And he did this without the benefit of high school diploma. When he was sixteen years old, he couldn't take the chaotic home life anymore, so he ran off and joined the Merchant Marines. My father spent the next five years traveling all over the world and learning how to work on high pressure boilers. The old man loved his life at sea until a Nazi U-Boat sent two torpedoes into the side of his ship in the North Atlantic. He escaped unscathed and was picked up by a British destroyer, believing that the close call would be his only brush with war. He was sadly mistaken when after returning to New York City to begin a new life he was drafted into the Army at the start of the Korean War. The old man always said that the only good thing he got out of that war was Nick Palmeri.

As a high school dropout back in Queens, my father's career options were limited. He worked for a few years as a messenger until he made a life changing discovery – civil service. Because of the high-pressure boiler license he received in the Merchant Marines, the old man qualified to take the civil service exam for stationery fireman. He passed the test and got hired by the Sanitation Department to maintain their incinerators. Nick also had been bitten by the civil service bug and ended up with a job as a sewer inspector.

I loved the old man, but there was something magical about the man I came to call Uncle Nick. My old man and Nick made similar salaries, but Nick always seemed to have the things everyone wanted. Nick always had a new car and would have me screaming with delight when he would whip out first row tickets right behind the Yankees dugout. I never asked how he was able to get the cars and the tickets. I was just thrilled to be riding in Uncle Nick's car with the old man on the way to Yankee Stadium.

Then one day when I was seventeen years old, everything changed. The smiling face of Uncle Nick was no longer a fixture sitting on my front stoop with the old man sipping cans of Rheingold. Something had happened, but no one was talking. If I even broached the subject of Uncle Nick with my mother or father, the conversation was quickly changed.

It was in my optometrist's office on Northern Boulevard that I learned the truth. I began wearing glasses when I was thirteen and every year my mother insisted that I get my eyes checked to see if my vision was getting worse – which it was. It turned out that my eyesight was the only thing about me that was not "average." I was average height and weight and my grades throughout my school years were average. I possessed average athletic ability and came from an average middle-class family. One of the few aspects of my life that was not average was my vision, which was below average.

The crowded waiting room meant I was in for a very long wait to see the doctor, so I reached to the scuffed wooden table next to my chair and grabbed the top magazine lying on top of a sloppy pile of periodicals. I was holding the latest issue of New York Magazine and when I opened to the first story my eyes widened as if the doctor had already dilated them. I couldn't believe what I was looking at. It was a story all about Uncle Nick.

Nick had been brought in for questioning by investigators because he had been observed hanging out in bars for an average of six hours a day when he should have been working. The investigators were astounded by Nick's excuse for being in the bars. Nick said that inspecting the sewer work of contractors was pointless because he and every other sewer inspector automatically approved the plumbing contractor's work in return for a few bucks. To Nick, taking those payoffs had become so routine that it never occurred to him that it would not be a good idea to use it as an excuse for being in the bars.

The article went on to say that Uncle Nick's attitude toward graft was well founded and was typical of an alarmingly large number of city workers. Prosecutors feared that thousands of city workers had come to accept payoffs as daily fringe benefits of their jobs.

My mouth hung open as wide as my eyes as I read how sanitation workers were regularly soliciting five dollars to take bedsprings and old furniture along with household garbage, and typists at a busy Department of Buildings office were so open about taking money that they placed dishes and jars near their desks – a reminder to building permit applicants that contributions were accepted. The article went on to highlight a long list of city workers who were arrested and convicted for taking bribes. But what about Uncle Nick? The story began with his arrest, and I hoped I was not going to be left in suspense – I wasn't.

The article said that after Nick confessed to taking money from plumbing contractors, he was offered immunity if he would assist in the investigation of the contractors. For six weeks Nick wore a body recorder and played a key role in the investigation. Arrests of plumbing contractors and other sewer inspectors and electrical inspectors were made, but Uncle Nick never went back to work. He had 24-years on the job when this all occurred, and he applied for his pension and retired. Uncle Nick felt he couldn't go back to work, a sentiment I didn't understand at the time. What I also didn't understand was why there were no more rides in new cars to Yankee Stadium anymore. In fact, there was no more contact with Uncle Nick. We still were next door neighbors, but we might as well have been a hundred miles away. My old man never said another word to Nick, and he smacked me in the back of the head when he saw me wave to him.

When I came home from the optometrist's office, I went directly into the kitchen where my father was sitting, nursing a Rheingold. I excitedly told him about the article I had read and how I wanted to understand everything that had transpired with Uncle Nick. The old man put his beer down on the table and stared at the wall clock while stroking his chin. He appeared to be searching for just the right words. Finally, he turned 45-degrees in his chair to face me. He took a deep breath and placed his hand on my shoulder. "Son, there are bad people in this world. There are murderers, rapists, child molesters and thieves. But the worst thing you can ever be is a rat!"

Our eyes remained locked and slowly I began to nod. I understood.

...

I remember the precise moment I decided I wanted to be a cop. It was during a late summer heat wave in New York City in 1970. It was the type of day that as an adult I learned to despise. New York City heat is not timid, and during these hot, sticky, miserable days I would find myself constantly drinking water in an attempt to keep up with the sweat flowing freely from every pore on my body. But that misery was the learned behavior of an adult. For a twelve-year-old kid in Jackson Heights, Queens, the weather wasn't important. All that mattered was that it was still summer vacation from school.

This particular summer was unique because it was the summer of "the game with the bat." I know what you're thinking – isn't the game with the bat called baseball? Technically, you'd be correct, but for my friends the story was not that simple. Early in the summer, Billy Blandino's dad had taken him to Shea Stadium to see the Met's play the Pirates, and the next day Billy appeared on the block holding a souvenir bat his old man had bought for him. It was a wooden Hillerich & Bradsby Tommy Agee model, but it wasn't a real bat, it was a miniature model about eighteen inches long.

With nothing to do, Billy, Kevin Harkins, Larry Kosco, and I roamed the streets trying to club each other with the bat. Finally, after several bruises were inflicted on a few arms, Larry suggested that we use the bat in a ballgame. Kevin immediately scoffed at the notion and pointed out that the first time the bat made contact with a real baseball it would shatter into a million pieces, but Larry was not dissuaded. He explained that we could go into the alley behind our homes and use a rubber ball to play the game.

The four of us lived on adjoining blocks that were connected by a community driveway. All the houses on my block were attached bungalows, so the community driveway allowed residents to access their backyards and garages. With an overhead view the driveway looked like a giant "capital I." Residents could enter the driveway from all four corners of the block to get to the rear driveway and garage in their homes. We could care less about the accessibility for cars. For kids, the community driveway was a perfect playground. Over the years, the driveway, which we called "the alley" was the site of countless games, of tag, manhunt, and football. And now, a new game was added to the list. It was brilliant in its simplicity. All that was needed was a pitcher, a catcher, and a batter. I dragged an old doormat out of my garage to use as home plate, Larry produced a Pensie Pinky rubber ball to go along with his miniature bat and it was game on. The game was like stickball – but it wasn't. It was also like baseball – but it wasn't. The game received its name organically. Several times a week during that summer when we were looking for something to do, someone would chirp, "Hey, let's play the game with the bat."

The playing field for the game with the bat was carefully chosen. The entire community driveway was only about twenty feet wide, which was perfect dimensions when the pitcher was the only fielder in the game. The location for the doormat home plate was designated at the end of the driveway where cars could turn left or right to exit to the street. This location allowed for a built-in backstop to our batter's box. If we located home plate anywhere else, much of the game would be spent chasing wild pitches several hundred yards down the driveway.

With our set up, most errant throws would be blocked by the fence and gate of a home's backyard and driveway. Our only problem was that the fence and gate we relied on as a backstop belonged to Foster the Fossil.

Walter Foster was 68-years, but to a twelve-year-old kid he might as well have been 108. The Fossil was a miserable old coot whose sole passion in life seemed to be watching to see when we were assembled in the driveway and then bursting out his back door to scream for us to be quiet and go somewhere else to play. If yelling at my crew was his enjoyment, the game with the bat provided a whole new level of gratification. Even though the Fossil's backyard fence and gate provided a suitable backstop for our game, those barriers were only four feet high, so at least three or four times a game a wild pitch or foul tip would bounce over the fence and into his yard. At that moment a new game began. It was called, "Beat the Fossil to the ball." When the game with the bat was new, we could always beat the Fossil to the ball, but as time went on and he became accustomed to our game, he would position himself just inside his back door, and no sooner did the ball bounce into his yard, Fossil was out the door, snatching the ball and bringing it into his house. The first time the Fossil grabbed our ball, it ended the game, but Kevin was determined to make it the last time. After ensuring that we all had a quarter Kevin led us on a hike to McClaren's Five & Ten cent store on Northern Boulevard.

"I was in here last week with my mom," Kevin said, "and I saw it."

"Saw what?" I asked.

"You'll see," Kevin nodded.

Kevin led the way through the entrance and to the third aisle. A huge grin covered his face as he stopped and pointed. "Look!"

Halfway down the aisle in the middle of the floor was a huge box filled with rubber balls. On the side of the box was a handwritten sign – 5 CENTS EACH.

Kevin put his right hand out with his palm up. "Ante up your quarters," he said. "Let the Fossil take our balls. We'll get twenty of them and keep him running until he has a heart attack."

We all picked up five balls to bring to the cashier. When I took hold of the first ball it became apparent why they were only 5-cents. Unlike the Spaldings and Pensie-Pinkies that usually cost a quarter each, these had to be the softest, flimsiest rubber balls I had ever held. I felt that if I squeezed too hard the ball might come apart. It didn't matter, however. No matter how cheap these balls were, they would keep the game with the bat going despite the Fossil's intervention.

July turned to August and the Fossil continued to devour our rubber balls, so much so that we had to make a second trip to McClaren's. Then one hot, steamy, Thursday afternoon it all came to a head. Once again, a wild pitch found its way into the Fossil's yard, and once again he was out his back door and on it instantly. I had been pitching at the time and I called for Kevin to toss me a fresh ball. Instead of tossing me a ball, Kevin motioned for the three of us to gather around him.

"What's up?" I asked.

"It's time for the Fossil to get a special delivery," Kevin smiled.

"What are you talking about?" Larry inquired.

"Look," Kevin said, as he produced a rubber ball from his pocket. This ball was different, however. It had been neatly sliced in half. "Follow me," Kevin directed.

He led the three of us out of the alley and crouched next to the curb. There were no pooper scooper laws at that time so dog poop could be found all along the curb. Kevin grabbed a nearby discarded popsicle stick and pushed a lump of poop inside one piece of his cut rubber ball. He then placed the other half of the ball on top, concealing the poop inside.

"What are you going to do?" I asked.

"Watch," Kevin said as he pulled a small bottle of super glue from his pocket and carefully applied a bead of glue around the perimeter of the ball, gluing it back into one solid unit. "We'll just let this sit for about thirty minutes and then the Fossil will get his special delivery."

Two more innings of the game with the bat were completed before Kevin held up both hands and announced, "It's time!"

Kevin went to the pitcher's mound and lobbed the "special" ball high over Larry's head so that it easily made it over the fence. Instantly, the back door opened, and Fossil snatched the ball before returning to his lair.

There was a momentarily lull in the action in the driveway until Kevin broke the silence. "That should teach the old bastard!"

We all laughed and the game with the bat resumed. During the next 45-minutes we managed to complete four innings without losing another ball to the Fossil. I was stepping up to bat and after taking a few practice swings with the miniature bat, I readied myself to receive Larry's pitch. Just before he began his wind up, I stepped back and raised my hand to halt Larry's pitching process. Something had caught my eye and required my undivided attention. Slowly making its way down the driveway was a New York City police car. The presence of the police on my block was an event. No one ever called for police intervention. There was very little property crime, and if families were having problems, they kept it to themselves and never got the police involved. The cops had not been in the driveway for more than thirty seconds when scores of neighbors began filling the driveway to see what was happening.

No one had exited the police vehicle when the Fossil was out his door holding a box in his hands. The driver of the police car remained inside the vehicle while the passenger exited and went to meet the Fossil. The cop was tall and wide, and walked with a strut like he owned the world.

"What's the problem, sir?" the cop said as he approached the Fossil.

"See," Fossil blurted. "Look what these little bastards throw in my yard."

It was now clear what the fossil was holding in the box – all the rubber balls he had snatched during the summer.

"Have they broken anything?" the cop yawned.

"Well, no," the Fossil stammered, "but they throw these things all over my grass."

"Grass?" the cop snickered, "you got nothing but weeds in your yard."

The Fossil held up his index finger and backed toward his door. "Just wait and see what they did today." He appeared a few seconds later holding what I believed was the "special" ball. Fossil pushed the ball up to the cop's nose. "See how bad this smells," Fossil said. "I think they're trying to poison me."

"Get that away from me," the cop said as he grabbed the ball away from the Fossil. When he squeezed the ball, the glued pieces came apart, so instead of having a rubber ball in his hand, the cop was holding a lump of dog poop.

"What the ..." the cop yelled as he threw the poop to the ground. "Do you think this is funny?" he snarled at the Fossil.

The Fossil shook his head vigorously. "No, no, officer," he stuttered. "It's not me – it's them."

The cop pointed a menacing finger at the Fossil. "Look Mac, the next time you call me here for nonsense like this I'm gonna give you a summons." He pointed to the box of rubber balls. "Now give the kids their balls back before I see if they want to press charges against you for petty larceny."

The Fossil handed the box of balls to the cop and retreated into his house, mumbling under his breath all the way. The cop turned to Larry, "Here kid," he said as he handed over the box. Just before he disappeared back into his police car, the big cop made eye contact with me and winked. And then they were gone. From that moment on I wanted to be a cop.

CHAPTER 1:

June 1981 – 1 A.M.: The Jolly Swagman was a classic dive bar. The interior of the neighborhood gin mill looked something like the interior of a coffin. The wallpaper was a dark burgundy with a strange shine to it. Either the shine was part of the effect, or no one had cleaned the place for the last twenty years or so and the smell of stale beer and nicotine was dominant. The dim light helped to camouflage the stained, worn wood bar that ran about 25-feet in length. Across from the bar were four equally worn wood tables bordering the wall. That was the extent of the décor. Framed photos and posters adorning the wall behind the bar indicated no particular theme, as the likes of Mickey Mantle, John Lennon, a Long Island Railroad Diesel Locomotive, Batman, and the famous Anheuser Busch print of Custer's Last Stand were prominently featured. The Swagman was for men who wanted to drink. For those suffering from hunger pangs between shots there might be a basket of stale pretzels on the bar. The only other alternative was to run next door to China Joe's and bring a takeout order back to the bar.

By 1981 Pete Flynn, the owner, of the Swagman, was being squeezed, figuratively and literally. Irish pubs, with full menus and live entertainment were becoming the rage throughout New York City, threatening the existence of the local neighborhood watering hole, especially in the borough of Queens. Two blocks north of the Swagman was Bridies and two blocks to the south Kate Cassidy's had recently opened its doors. With no food and the only entertainment being a Space Invaders arcade game wedged between a juke box that seldom worked and a cigarette machine that worked even less, the Swagman was slowly being squeezed to death. Sure, there were still nights that the bar was full, but the norm had become just like this Friday night that had recently transitioned into Saturday morning.

The juke box was out of order again making the rhythmic mechanical tones of the Space Invaders machine the only competition for the conversations at the bar. The video game didn't have much trouble dominating the environment. There were only six patrons at opposite ends of the bar to occupy Pete's attention. At one end Joe Donovan sat silently staring into his partially filled glass as if the drink was having a hypnotic effect on him. Andy Miller sat next to him rambling on about the sad state of the world, oblivious to the fact that Joe wasn't listening to a word he said. At eighty years of age, Andy was twice Joe's age, and after Joe had a few drinks, Andy had more pep to his step than his younger friend. Andy was short, thin, and still vibrant at his advanced age, with an acerbic tongue that carried an opinion about everything. He had lived in the apartment building across Woodhaven Boulevard for over fifty years, and his main activity since retiring from the NYC Transit Authority thirty years earlier was drinking at the Jolly Swagman.

Kevin Harkins, Billy Blandino, and Larry Kosco sat at the bar draining bottles of Michelob. I pushed a dollar bill forward on the bar for the tenth time during the evening. "Four quarters, please," I requested.

Pete slid the coins along the bar and into my hand. I pushed back my stool and made a tenth trip to the Space Invaders machine. I had become addicted to the game and had come within a thousand points of getting my name on the machine for high score. I just was not going to quit until my name was on the screen for everyone to see, no matter how much it cost me. Blasting the aliens during the early stages of the game had become very easy, so I didn't mind the distraction of Andy's comments.

"With the amount of money you pour into that machine," Andy laughed, "Pete's not gonna have to worry about the pubs putting him out of business."

"Maybe," I replied as I kept tapping the button that fired an alien killing ray.

"I thought you boys were taking the police test in the morning." Andy said.

"We are," I said.

"Well," Andy snickered, "It's morning. Why are you jerks still in here drinking?"

"We'll be alright," I said as I increased my concentration on the game.

"Yeah, don't worry about us," Kevin called out. "Anyway, isn't it after your bedtime, Methuselah?"

"That's a good one," Larry chuckled as he slapped Kevin's back.

Joe Donovan broke free from his trance and shifted his stare from his glass to me. "Andy's right," he mumbled. "You should go home, Jimmy, and get some sleep before you take that test."

"That's right, Murphy." Andy blurted. Joe had returned to staring into his glass as Andy placed his hand on his shoulder. "You need to listen to him," he urged. "This is a smart fucking man. He's an instructor at the police academy and knows what he's talking about."

I had come up short again as GAME OVER filled the screen. I strolled back to my friends and shrugged. "Joe's probably right. We should get out of here."

"Why should we get out of here?" Kevin snapped. "Because the smart fucking man said so." Kevin sipped his beer and smirked. "Some smart fucking man. He's a transit cop who teaches other transit cops. Besides that, he spends all his time drunk at the other corner of the bar."

"Lay off, Kevin," Larry warned.

"What's your problem?" Kevin shot back.

"Joe's a good guy, and he hasn't had it easy," Billy said.

"What are you talking about?" Kevin asked.

"Joe's wife and kid were killed by a drunk driver about five years ago."

"Yeah, I heard about that," I said.

Kevin sighed, "I never heard about that."

"Well, I'm getting out of here," I declared.

"Me too," Larry said

"Wait for me," Kevin moaned.

I pushed a five-dollar bill forward on the bar. "Good night, Pete," I said.

"Good luck on the test," Pete called.

"Yeah," Andy laughed as he pointed to Kevin. "I hope you do better than last time."

"Screw you, grandpa," Kevin snarled as he pushed through the door.

Andy's dig at Kevin involved the Transit Police Officer test that had been given three months earlier. I had no desire to be a transit cop, so I skipped the test. Kevin, Billy, and Larry took the exam and Larry and Billy did well and were on the eligible list, even though they also had no desire to be transit cops. Kevin had been thrown out of the school when the proctor accused him of cheating by looking at the paper of the test taker next to him. Kevin shrugged off his cheating scandal by rationalizing that he never wanted to be a transit cop anyway.

I was always successful at school, when I wanted to be. My average grades required very little effort and by the time I was in college C's had become the normal grade as I drank and dozed my way through John Jay College of Criminal Justice. Still, even with a 2.4 GPA, I possessed the same freshly minted bachelor's degree as those with a 4.0 GPA. I also turned out to be a good test taker, which was an essential skill in the world of civil service competitive examinations.

Even though we had been stupid enough to stay out sucking down beers until after midnight, the NYPD test was a big deal for my crew. It was the first NYPD test to be given in over six years.

U.S. economic stagnation in the 1970s hit New York City particularly hard, amplified by a large movement of middle-class residents to the suburbs, which drained the city of tax revenue. New York City was on the brink of bankruptcy. On July 1, 1975, the City of New York laid off an initial 15,000 workers, including 3,000 cops and 1,600 firefighters – 20% of the city's entire force. Some 26 fire companies were simply disbanded. By September, 45,000 workers had been laid off. From July 1975 until November 1979, no police officers were hired or trained in the City of New York. The only "new" officers were those who had been laid off on July 1, 1975, and were rehired over the next three years. With all the laid off officers rehired and the city slowly regaining its financial footing, an NYPD open competitive civil service examination finally offered hope to the wannabe cops of my crew.

I was up bright and early with no effects from the beer I had imbibed. I was on my own as I drove to Cardoza High School in Bayside. The other members of my crew had been assigned different schools in Queens and Manhattan. I found the test very easy, but of course Kevin was the only one to state that he probably aced the test with a score of 100%. It would be weeks before we would receive the test results in the mail, so we returned to our lives of working and hanging out at the Swagman.

Work for me was with the New York City Criminal Justice Agency. I was excited to get a job in the criminal justice system, but I quickly learned to despise my job. Everyone arrested in New York City must be brought before a judge and arraigned within 72-hours, although the vast majority of arrestees were arraigned within 24-hours. At the arraignment, the judge informed the arrestee of the charges and decided whether to grant bail, hold the arrestee without bail, or release the arrestee on his own recognizance. This last option was known as an R.O.R., and it was my job to conduct R.O.R. interviews to provide the judge with information regarding whether the arrestee would be a good risk for R.O.R. The position sounded somewhat impressive, but in reality, a monkey could have done the job. I asked four questions based on how long they resided in their current residence and their employment status and history. Based on the answers a certain number of points was assigned to each answer. When the points were added up, they would fit into the categories of highly recommended for ROR, recommended for ROR, or not recommended for ROR.

It was all objective, and I had no input in making a recommendation. The point total alone determined the recommendation received. This job that any simpleton could do was performed in a horrible environment. I originally liked the idea of working inside Queens Central Booking. Every borough in the city had a central booking location where all arrested persons were brought for their initial booking. In Queens, Central Booking was inside the 112th Precinct in Forest Hills. I liked the idea of being around cops, and for the most part, they were good guys and treated me well. Not surprisingly, my problems were with the prisoners.

I worked in a small office behind the desk sergeant. Actually, "office" is not the right word to describe my work area. It was more like a small desk jammed into a closet. Whenever prisoners came in from the precincts I would go to the cells and conduct my interviews through the bars. I was required to wear a shirt and tie so when I appeared outside the cell with a clipboard in hand, the prisoners automatically assumed I was a lawyer and their disappointment in learning the truth was sometimes manifested in a stream of spit, punches, and even an attempt at strangulation. The strangulation attempt was partly my own fault because it had never occurred to me to wear clip on ties. The day after I was gurgling with my reddened face pressed against the bars, my dresser drawer was filled with clip on ties.

I pulled into the community driveway and left my car idling while I opened my driveway gate. Up ahead, I watched the current generation of Fossil ballbreakers playing hockey. I wondered how many rolls of electrical tape the Fossil had collected.

The day at Central Booking had seemed particularly long and taxing, and even though it was Friday, I had already made the decision to stay home and watch TV instead of meeting my friends at the Swagman.

"Hey, pop," I sighed as I walked into the kitchen and opened the refrigerator door. "What's new?"

My dad was sitting at the kitchen table watching TV. Even though he had a color TV and a comfortable easy chair in the living room, he chose to always sit on a hard chair at the kitchen table and squint at the screen of a 13-inch black & white television.

He kept his back facing me as he answered. "This is the only thing new," he said as he held an envelope above his head.

"What is it?" I asked as I took the first sip from the can of Coke.

"Come get it," he responded.

I snatched the envelope and froze momentarily. It was the result of the police exam. I took a deep breath and tore open the envelope.

I was still facing my dad's back. "Well?" he said.

I gulped before replying. "99." I repeated the score with a bit more steam. "I got 99 on the test."

"That's great," my dad said as he spun in his chair to face me. "I have a question for you."

"What?"

"What are you gonna do about these?" he said as he leaned forward and tapped a lens on my glasses with his index finger.

"What do you mean?" I asked.

"I think you know what I mean," he sighed. "You have to have no worse than 20/40 uncorrected vision to get on the NYPD. What's your vision?"

"I'm not sure," I whispered.

"But you are sure it's worse than 20/40, right?"

"I guess so," I shrugged.

My dad turned back to his small television.

I shook my head. "Geez, A moment ago I was feeling great. Thanks for raining on my parade."

Again, he spun back to face me. "Look, I just don't want you to be disappointed. You have to face the reality of that vision requirement."

"Hey, Kevin wears glasses too," I shot back.

My dad chuckled. "Kevin has been running angles since he was six years old. I'll guarantee you he knows someone who is in a position to get him through that vision test. Do you know anyone like that?"

My silence was the only answer my dad needed. "I didn't think so," he said.

"Well, if Kevin does have some scam worked out," I said, "maybe he can bring me in on it."

My dad shook his head. "Trust me, scams like that don't work on the buddy system. If Kevin has it worked out, the angle will be for Kevin, and Kevin alone."

"So, what should I do?"

"Move forward when you get called for the physical and medical tests," he said. "Just don't be shocked if you can't get past the vision test."

"Okay," I said as I began moving out of the kitchen.

"Wait a minute," he called.

I spun around in the doorway between the kitchen and living room to see my dad holding up the Chief civil service newspaper. He was pointing to the headline on the first page that read, FILING TO OPEN FOR SANITATION EXAM. "You might want to file for this exam," he said.

"A garbageman," I scoffed. "I'm a college graduate and you want me to be a garbageman."

"Since when did you become so high and mighty," he huffed. "It's a secure civil service job with pay and benefits almost identical to the NYPD. All I'm saying is that there's no vision requirement to be a sanitation man, so it might be an option for you." He shrugged and turned back to the TV. "But if it's beneath you, then forget about it."

Everything my dad said turned out to be true. I failed the vision portion of the NYPD medical exam while my buddies passed. Just like the old man predicted, Kevin's uncle, who was a PBA delegate, reached out to the cop from the Medical Division who was giving the vision tests on the day of Kevin's appointment, and amazingly, Kevin read the chart for the 20/40 requirement. My father was also correct about my other option. I took the Sanitation exam and scored 100%. Now, we sat in the Swagman sipping our beers while Billy, Larry, and Kevin went on non-stop about when they were going to be called for the NYPD.

The four of us had been together since the first grade. From CYO baseball and basketball to the boy scouts, we did everything together. We all wanted to be cops too, although our reasons were different. I was motivated to the NYPD because of the Fossil story, and Larry's old man was on the job. Kevin's uncle was the PBA delegate who pulled strings to get him through the vision test. Billy was a follower and went along with what the rest of us were doing, including wanting to join the NYPD.

Kevin was the most outgoing of the crew, and the quickest witted. While Billy and Larry shared my average physical traits, Kevin was always bigger. What I didn't know until many years later was that part of the reason Kevin was bigger than the rest of my crew was because he was a year older. Kevin had been left back in the first grade, so when I met Kevin, he was making his second attempt at getting through the first grade. I'm still not sure how it was possible to fail first grade, but Kevin had managed to do it.

As adults, Kevin was still bigger than me, and he seemed to have snide remarks for every occasion that kept everyone laughing. He also had a bit of a mean streak in him which I never gave a second thought until that mean streak affected me.

I had involuntarily assumed the role of an outsider. With the barstool conversations revolving almost exclusively around their upcoming appointments to the NYPD, I would have welcomed some empathy and at least an attempt to bring me into the conversation. Billy and Larry were good about it, but Kevin seemed to relish the opportunity to point out the fact that I was not part of their inner circle anymore. They were waiting to be called to become New York's Finest while I sat alone at the bar pondering my future as a garbageman. I have to admit that I resented the fact that Kevin had been able to scam his way through the NYPD vision test while I was left out in the cold. A radical thought entered my mind. What would happen if I "dropped a dime" on Kevin by sending a letter to the police commissioner informing him all about Kevin's fake vision test? That question would remain unanswered. I could never send that letter and become my old man's definition of the worst thing in the world – a rat!

Even though I had taken the sanitation test almost two months after the NYPD exam, I ended up getting appointed to the Department of Sanitation only a week after Larry, Billy and Kevin were sworn into the NYPD. It wasn't particularly odd that all three of my friends were in the first class appointed from the civil service list because the academy class was huge.

They didn't stay late, but Billy, Larry and Kevin still found time to strut their stuff in the Swagman during that first week after they were hired. They went on and on about how a total of 3500 recruits had been hired, including 2700 NYPD, 500 Transit Police, and 300 Housing. They said the class was so big that all the new recruits could not be hired on the same day, leaving some recruits with Monday as their date of hire while several hundred had Tuesday as the day they entered the department. Kevin's mean-spirited nature again presented itself as he went on ad nauseum about how he had seniority over Larry and Billy because he was processed for a Monday hiring date while Larry and Billy were processed on Tuesday.

At one point I was able to get Billy alone while Kevin rambled on about his three-day career with the NYPD at the other end of the bar.

"Sounds like it's been a crazy three days," I noted.

Billy shook his head and chuckled. "It was insanity out at Brooklyn College."

"How so?" I asked.

Billy grabbed a handful of peanuts from the basket on the bar. "People were coming from all different city jobs to be hired by the NYPD. The auditorium was packed and every minute or so a cop would get on a microphone and ask who was currently in the transit police academy, who was an active transit cop in the field, who was a bus driver, who was a correction officer in their academy. It went on and on, and as people would stand up to identify themselves as in one of the groups called on the microphone, cops from the Applicant Investigation Division would run over to them and ask them questions and give them additional paperwork. It was crazy."

"Sounds like it," I agreed.

"It gets better," Billy continued. "After three days at Brooklyn College we finally were broken into companies and told to report to the police academy on 20th Street in Manhattan. The first instructor into our classroom that morning was a big, fat sergeant who looked like he had at least twenty years on the job. He didn't introduce himself, and instead began ranting about how the department was not prepared to handle a recruit class of 3500 and in order to staff the academy with instructors they transferred a group of new sergeants like him to become instructors. He said he had never requested assignment to the police academy and had no teaching experience. He took a deep breath and said welcome to the NYPD and good luck – you'll need it."

When I departed the Swagman Kevin had to take a parting shot. "Hey Jimmy," he chuckled, "make sure you check your mail when you go home. You may have gotten your appointment notice as a garbageman today. You'll recognize the envelope immediately – it will be the one with flies circling it."

I could still hear the laughter from inside the bar long after the door closed behind me.

As fate would have, Kevin was prophetic – almost. My appointment notice to the Sanitation Department arrived the next day and there were no flies near the envelope.

...

Rose-gold light was falling onto Jamaica Bay and sea gulls passed overhead on another beautiful morning at Floyd Bennett Field in Brooklyn, a far reach of New York City mostly devoid of New Yorkers and cars. New Yorkers, at least the New Yorkers from my Jackson Heights neighborhood, tended to be very tribal. We stayed amongst our own tribe in our own village. Even though Floyd Bennett Field was in the neighboring borough of Brooklyn, I had never been there before and the only reason I was standing on the tarmac on the beautiful Wednesday morning was to begin my garbageman training.

I quickly discovered that there were many differences between garbage school and what my friends were experiencing at the police academy. There were not anywhere near 3500 trainees as there was in the police academy. My class consisted of 145 rookie garbagemen. There also seemed to be other training classes taking place in various stages of the one-month training course.

It was a perfect setting for learning how to drive a garbage truck, as the members of my group watched some of the world's least graceful vehicles groaning and screeching their way through a narrow trail of orange traffic cones. Nearby, where Sanitation Department trainees were learning how to both load the trucks and dump them, the air was filled with sounds familiar to any New Yorker — the crashing of cans and crushing of garbage in the early morning hours, so loud it might as well be happening inside my bedroom.

"Hey!" an instructor called out to his students. "You have to make sure the hopper's closed before you drive off!"

It was still only 6:30 A.M. as the sun burned off the ocean mist. I milled about with my new classmates staring at the activity in the distance. Suddenly, I had a new interest in the familiar gaping hole into which workers fed trash bags — as it slowly closed shut with a satisfying clank. The hulking blade that compacts the trash moved in a single, sweeping motion. We watched with quiet concentration. Over the sound of the rusty metal, the man operating the truck, in black sunglasses and a crew cut, yelled: "Garbage goes in, then what goes out?" In unison, the class standing near the truck shouted, "Juice!"

A few weeks later I learned that trash juice, the viscous concoction brewed by the contents of every truck, and its habit of spraying out of bags as they're compacted, is a major theme at the Department of Sanitation's training academy.

"You'll get your turn," An instructor with a bushy beard said as he directed my group to a series of large trailers on the west side of the field.

The first day was an exercise in completing what seemed like an endless flow of paperwork along with a history lesson. With my wrist still aching from all the forms I filled out I welcomed the walk down memory lane provided by the bushy bearded instructor.

His name was Instructor Dominguez, and he said the Sanitation Department's training academy was created in 1950, but that there had been formal efforts to train new workers since the early 20th century, when the agency was known as the Department of Street Cleaning. He chuckled when he mentioned that picking up dead horses and stopping cholera were no longer concerns.

Instructor Dominguez said the job could be about as gross as you could imagine. He rattled off the most repulsive things he encountered on a route — a pig's head, an entire lamb, "disco rice," which was a deceptively appetizing name for maggots. Still, he shrugged and said it was a great job, with good pay and benefits, union protection, and a clear path to a middle-class life in the city. Dominguez said there was a pension, and opportunities for overtime and promotion. He said the hardest part of the job was the schedule, which could be erratic in early years.

Instructor Dominguez said that we owed a lot to those who came before us. He said that for decades, sanitation workers made far less than city cops and firefighters and worked in dangerous conditions without sick time and for lower pensions. But in February of 1968, the department's 10,000 uniformed workers went on a wildcat strike, led by their union founder and president John DeLury. Tens of thousands of pounds of trash accumulated over a week, with a major snowstorm threatening to bury it all. The union won, securing better wages and benefits.

Dominguez said that years later we were reaping the benefits because a job with the department now meant saving up for a house, good insurance, and a respected career. He emphasized that in twenty years a sanman, which was the department jargon for sanitation man, could begin drawing a pension.

"I haven't had a bad day on the job yet," Dominguez grinned, "and in three more years I'll be in West Palm Beach sipping a Mai tai."

My classmates were a diverse group. Besides those like me who were beginning their first career job, I had classmates who had been corrections officers, teachers, photojournalists, and UPS drivers. The stories of what brought them to the sanitation department were similar: too few or too many hours, bad pay, layoffs. One told me he made his son take the test with him and now his son was being processed in one of the other trailers. Another classmate told me he took the test in high school because his dad was a DSNY worker.

On that first day I couldn't imagine why training to be a garbageman would require a full month, but in retrospect, I found that a month wasn't adequate to cover all the required topics.

The basic training included everything from defensive driving to fitting snow chains on tires. The trash truck obstacle course was the event everyone looked forward to. Orange traffic cones were set up around the field to imitate a tight street circuit. A row of white sanitation trucks were at the ready as a group of trainees stood in a huddle around the instructors. Shabbir Suhal, another instructor and former accountant, prepped the class, warning us not to hit the cones, which he called "my kids and future Nobel laureates."

The rest of the trucks began moving around the tarmac, like the world's slowest go-kart race. I watched as most people hit a cone or two and silently wept for Suhal's fallen Nobel laureates. As the month of training progressed, the obstacle course got more difficult to better mimic a chaotic city street. The navigation was hard, and I incurred Suhal's wrath when I knocked over two cones.

During one training day my class was assembled at different stations — most of them trucks — positioned around the old airfield. Because there was no actual garbage in the training field, we had to imagine bags of trash and piles of disassembled furniture as we went through the motions of loading the trucks. We rotated between three different vehicles — a front-loading E-Z pack that hoists dumpsters, a salt spreader for snow control, and the regulation white sanitation truck used for trash collections. My classmate Leon Haynes dutifully listened to the instructors' every word as he prepared for his turn with me as his partner. We briefly conferred, agreeing that the spreader was the easiest. When we got to the collection truck, an instructor pulled the lever and the tailgate lifted. Suddenly, a brackish liquid the consistency of spittle poured out, and we stepped back to avoid the splash. Recalling what we observed on our first day of training Leon said, "Juice," pointing to the trail of liquid on the ground. "Juice," I repeated solemnly.

Next up was baskets training, where we learned how to pick up and empty the city-issued corner trash cans. The maneuver seemed simple enough — pick up a basket, tip it, bang it a few times to knock loose any straggler trash, then close the hopper by pulling a lever. I tried lifting one. Even empty, it easily weighed 30 pounds. My heart raced and my arms trembled. After I had tipped it into the truck, I was instructed to drop it rather than set it down to expend less energy, which meant almost crushing my toes, something I forgot I had also been instructed to carefully avoid. Now, the instructor said to imagine doing that 400-times on a single route. I did not want to imagine that.

We then ran through things to watch out for on the job: bent license plates will slice up your knees, tow hitches on trucks will bruise your shins. We were advised to avoid steel-toed boots, since they won't stop a truck from crushing your foot and the metal might slice your toes off. Instructor Dominguez, at one point, handed around a gory photo of a huge leg gash he got from a sharp object hidden in a trash bag.

Safety was emphasized in every training topic. Police work involves occupational dangers, but trash pickup ranks among OSHA's list of occupations with the highest fatal work injuries. There's heavy machinery and the unpredictability of New York City streets, where drivers run amok. But there's also the slow deterioration that comes with the intense physical labor. Over the years, bodies that must lift and carry all that weight — bend and contort and move — wear down. Safety, maybe even more than trash juice, is the heart of the training. Sanitation employees often work in twos and threes and the training emphasizes that partnership is a foundational principle in the department.

At a session devoted to cleaning up litter, instructor Suhal was teaching us about one of the department's biggest occupational hazards: syringes in trash bags.

"Do you have X-ray vision?" he asked. He warned the trainees to hold the bags away from their bodies. "There could be needles in there!"

Another instructor showed us how to line up the end of a snow chain with a forward-facing ridge on the tire, and then wind it around clockwise. He explained that once we went to work, we would need to learn how to do it quickly, because hunching over the tire of a truck carrying 16 tons of salt "isn't somewhere you want to be for too long."

From day one of training, my new friend Leon Haynes was obsessed with rats and how to avoid them. After three weeks Leon was disappointed to find that the training did not cover how to deal with rats. Finally, during a classroom session in a trailer, Leon raised his hand and asked Dominguez if he had any advice for avoiding rodent-related injuries.

Dominguez paused and then said, "Get a broom and tap the can."

The equipment that sanitation workers use is every bit as intricate as the gear on a fire engine. One day we were trained in how to work a front-end loader, which was used to move heavy materials, like snow, salt, dirt and other debris. Operating the vehicle requires manipulating three pedals, two levers and a steering wheel that controls the body and front axle at once.

After spending the morning on the front-end loader, I sat in the lunch trailer with Leon Haynes. Leon became philosophical about the training he was receiving on all the different sanitation vehicles as he worked his way through an Italian combo hero. He said he used to work in shipping and receiving before finally getting the call from the Sanitation Department, seven years after taking the written test.

Leon said, "I used to have trucks like these ones under my Christmas tree when I was little. Now I get to play with the real thing."

I had dreamed about graduation day, but the dreams involved the police academy, not trash school. I had mixed feelings standing at attention on the tarmac of Floyd Bennet Field along with my classmates and instructors listening to the Sanitation Commissioner drone on about the vital job performed by the Sanitation Department. On one hand, the month of training had caused me to develop a newfound respect for the complexities of the skills required to perform the sanman job. On the other hand, I was still a garbageman.

The commissioner finally concluded his speech and one by one the graduates' received diplomas. The lead instructor shouted, "dismissed!" and the entire class cheered before drifting away to waiting friends and relatives.

If my parents were faking their enthusiasm, they were doing a good acting job. My dad grabbed my hand firmly and slapped my shoulder as he pulled me close for a congratulatory hug. My mom kissed me on the cheek and grabbed the diploma from my hand. She smiled and nodded as she examined the document. "I'm so proud of you Jimmy," she gushed.

Why shouldn't she be proud. Her son was now a certified garbageman.

My folks took me out for an early dinner at Donovan's Irish Pub, an institution in Queens. The Sanitation Department had been benevolent enough to grant its new sanmen the day after graduation off, so I swung by the Swagman for a few games of Space Invaders. My Friends had not even reached the halfway point in their police academy training class, so I was somewhat surprised to see Kevin holding court at the bar with a couple of cops from the 104th Precinct.

Kevin skipped all the preliminaries and got right to the main event. "Look who's here fresh from graduation," he called.

"What's up?" I said to the group at the bar as I headed straight for the video game. I was trying to concentrate on zapping aliens, but I couldn't help hearing Kevin in the background.

"Hey Pete," Kevin called to the bartender, "don't take the trash out tonight, Jimmy will do it. He's now a professional garbageman."

I had almost reached the breaking point with Kevin's taunts, but his ribbing suddenly became unimportant. I was on fire with the joystick and my score was inching ever closer to that magical high score. And then, it happened. I had obtained the high score on the machine. I probably spent close to five hundred dollars on that machine, but as JIMMY M flashed across the screen as the top score for everyone to see, every quarter was worth it. Kevin could rant all he wanted about professional garbagemen – at that moment as I took a long sip of Michelob and looked back at the screen flashing my name, all was right with the world.

The state of the world changed about a minute later. In a surreal scene that took no more than five minutes, two men entered the bar wheeling in a GALACTA arcade game on a hand truck. I couldn't believe my eyes when I saw them plug in the GALACTA game before unplugging Space Invaders and removing the game from the bar via the same hand truck. Pete signed some paperwork one of the men placed on the bar and they were gone, and so was Space Invaders and my immortalized name.

"Pete," I moaned. "How could you? I just got the high game on the screen a minute ago, and now the game is gone."

"Sorry," Pete shrugged. "I don't own the games and the owners change them up every now and then."

"Don't you have any control of what games you have in here?" I asked.

"Are you kidding?" Pete chuckled. "You know who owns all the vending machines and video games." Pete pushed the side of his nose with his index finger, a gesture indicating that organize crime was involved.

I was completely deflated, but just for good measure I had to endure a parting shot from Kevin. "I'll see you next week, buddy. I can't wait to hear some garbage war stories."

CHAPTER 2:

Two days later I awoke at 4 A.M. to begin what would become a routine for the next year. The Department of Sanitation is divided into 59 districts, and I was assigned to District 2 on Spring Street in Lower Manhattan. In department jargon the garage was simply called Manhattan two.

At 5:30 I was sitting around in the muster area of the garage watching my new colleagues drift in. At 6 A.M. a hulking uniformed Foreman whose beard and bushy hair made him look like he just came down from the mountains, entered the muster area to conduct roll call and announce the routes and assignments for the day.

I was assigned to work with Joe Recupero and Biju Thomas. Joe had been with the department for 33-years and Biju was nearing his 20th anniversary, although he had no intention of retiring anytime soon. Joe's family had been entrenched in Bensonhurst, Brooklyn for generations, while Biju emigrated from India, and two years after he landed in New York he was working as a sanman.

I feared that two senior men would resent having to drag around a rookie with them, but I couldn't have been more mistaken. The third man on their crew had only been on the job for a year when he was called for a job with the Fire Department, so they were used to having a rookie tagging along with them.

Joe fired up one of the big white collection trucks in the garage while Biju spoke to me by the garage entrance. "The regulations say we're supposed to rotate the driving duties," Biju began, "but on this crew, Joe drives. He's almost sixty years old and still wants to get a few more years out of the job."

"I understand," I nodded.

"Don't get me wrong," Biju continued, "Joe's in good shape. That's one of the benefits of this job. It forces you to stay in shape." He sighed, "But still, tossing cans behind the truck is no place for a sixty-year-old."

"I completely understand," I repeated.

"Good," Biju smiled and tapped my arm gently. "Besides, there are other benefits to being a collector. Welcome to the crew."

I was curious about these other benefits as I stood on a platform on the rear of the truck and clutched the handles tightly with both hands as Joe drove through the pre-dawn streets. The day's route included parts of Soho and Greenwich Village. When we reached the first block on the route it was still dark. "That's one of the little things I like about the job," Biju said as we tossed garbage bags into the hopper. "I like watching the city wake up."

I tossed garbage into the truck from private residences, schools, and non-profits. We did not take the trash from in front of stores. Businesses were required to pay a private company for trash removal, an issue that would become very important to me several years later.

On the second block on the route Biju noticed me standing directly behind the hopper. "Hey Jimmy," he called. "didn't they tell you about 'juice' during training? Always stand to the side of the hopper. We lost a guy a few years ago when acid sprayed out of the hopper and hit him directly in the face."

"Sorry," I sighed.

As the route continued the conversation turned social. "How do you think you're gonna like the 6 A.M. to 2 P.M. shift?" Biju asked.

"I don't know," I shrugged. "I'm not used to getting up this early."

"You'll learn to love it," Biju laughed. "I admit it's not great for a single guy, but you won't be single forever. I'm able to pick my kids up at school, go to the gym for a workout and be home for dinner by five o'clock. But you do have a point about getting up so early in the morning," Biju admitted. "Even after so many years on this shift there are some mornings I still want to throw my alarm clock out the window."

I had just tossed two heavy bags into the hopper when I was stunned by a shout emanating from the sidewalk on the other side of the street.

"When are you going back to India?"

"As soon as you go back to Mexico," Biju shot back. "Good morning, Diego," Biju said.

"Buenos Dias, amigo," Diego replied.

"Hey, Jimmy," Biju called, "this is Diego, the super of the building and one of our good friends on the route."

"It's a pleasure to meet you," I said. Even though it was my first day on the job I had enough sense to realize that a man tossing garbage into a truck should not offer a handshake."

"You've got good men with you," Diego said. "Learn from them."

"I will," I replied.

"Have a good day, Diego," Joe called from inside the truck as it began to roll forward.

"See you next time," Diego waved.

"He seems like a nice guy," I said.

"He is," Biju replied. "We meet a lot of nice people on the route, but then again, there are some things I wish we could avoid." Biju pointed to the stacks of plastic garbage bags piled on the sidewalk in front of the next apartment building. Specifically, he pointed to several rats moving in and out of the bags. "I hate those things, but unfortunately, they're a part of the job."

At ten o'clock Joe called out from the driver's seat. "It's time for a run. Hop on and I'll drop you off at the park."

I looked to Biju for an explanation.

"Just hang on and I'll explain when we get off," he said.

A few minutes later Biju and I were standing on the sidewalk in front of a city park while Joe's white truck disappeared in the distance to the north.

"I told you about the benefits of tossing cans," Biju said, "and this is one of them."

"What benefits?" I asked.

"The truck can only hold so many tons of compacted garbage and usually around this time during the shift, the driver has to take the truck way uptown to an incinerator to dump the load. Joe will be back in a little over an hour so we can finish the route. But while we wait..." Biju held up two paddles he had removed from the passenger cab of the truck. "Do you play paddleball," he asked.

"I don't play very often," I said.

"Well, that's about to change," Biju said as he handed me a paddle and led the way toward the handball courts.

A strange thought entered my mind. I might actually like this job.

...

I was never really going to get used to getting up at four o'clock in the morning, but on my first anniversary of joining the Sanitation Department I had to admit it had been a pretty good year. Since I was still living at home with my parents, my bank account was growing like the piles of garbage at a landfill. I also was very lucky to have spent the year on the crew with Joe and Biju, who accepted a rookie like me immediately and were the main reason I was actually enjoying picking up other people's garbage every day in lower Manhattan.

While on the route Biju and Joe would often chat with the residents they encountered, who were grateful for their service, and I had quickly joined in these conversations. I learned a lot about the different neighborhoods and the people who lived in them. I was always struck by how different neighborhoods could be that were only separated by a few blocks.

My first year on the job could not have gone better. Regrettably, I couldn't say the same thing about another area of my life. Maybe it was simply a case of jealously, but I became increasingly depressed over Kevin, Larry, and Billy. My three lifelong friends had graduated from the police academy and were now doing what I had dreamed of – working on the streets of New York as cops.

Billy was assigned to Midtown South, billed as the busiest police precinct in the world, while Larry was sent to the 62nd Precinct in Coney Island. As usual, Kevin worked an angle in getting his assignment. He worked a month of field training in a Neighborhood Stabilization Unit in Queens before his uncle was able to pull some strings and get him assigned to the Narcotics Division.

I never felt like more of an outsider socially. I considered Joe and Biju good friends, but they were work friends from completely different age groups. Biju had a wife and kids, and Joe was expecting his first grandchild. We weren't going to be hanging out after work together anytime soon. I was feeling more and more isolated from my friends. When we were at the Swagman, one hundred percent of the conversations revolved around the NYPD, a subject I had nothing to contribute to. Nobody except Kevin wanted to talk about the Department of Sanitation, and he was only interested in humiliating me with his endless snide remarks about garbage.

On increasingly frequent occasions I found myself alone at the Swagman's long dark bar. Kate Cassidy's, the pub on the next block had grown in popularity and had developed the reputation as a "cop bar." Kevin, Billy, and Larry began spending most of their time at Kate's, and whenever I joined them, Kevin wasted no time in announcing the presence of an outsider – a garbageman. Billy and Larry could see that my tolerance for Kevin's wise cracks was wearing thin. They reminded me that Kevin was just being the practical joker he had been since the first grade. They were right. Kevin was a classic practical joker, but the reality was that a practical joker was nothing more than a sadist who took delight in ridiculing and mocking a target. I had become Kevin's target.

...

It was so hot, my hair was lying like a second skin over my cheeks, my sweat making it look as if I were just caught in a sudden storm. I bent at the waist and readied myself to return the serve off the wall. I tried to bounce from side to side but my legs were empty and there was a rising feeling of nausea from my stomach. Just before I was ready to throw up a white flag, Biju turned from the service line and said, "It's too hot, let's go sit on the benches."

"If that's what you want," I shrugged, pretending I was ready to play for at least another hour.

Biju soaked his head in the water fountain before settling in on the wooden bench that was located in the delicious shade of several trees. I wet my head and neck, took a long drink, and made it to the bench before my legs gave out.

"Whew!" Biju huffed, "I'm getting too old to be playing in this heat."

"I guess that's what happens," I said, trying to mask the fact that I had been seconds away from passing out.

The familiar loud clanking and squeaking caused us both to look toward the street.

"Joe's back," Biju said.

"And he's not empty handed," I noted as I watched Joe approach carrying a white pizza box.

"What do you have there, Joey boy?" Biju sang.

"I figured you guys would be half dead from playing paddleball in this heat, so I stop by Carmine's and got us a pie." Joe dropped the box on the chessboard that was chiseled into the top of most concrete tables at city parks. He stood with his hands on his hips and shook his head. "And from the looks of you two, I was right."

"I was fine," Biju said, "but the kid wanted to stop."

"Sure, he did," Joe chuckled.

The two slices and cold soda were heavenly. I started moving off the bench, but Joe quickly stopped my progress.

"Relax, Jimmy," he cautioned, "we still got twenty minutes left on our meal period."

I slumped back in the bench, closed my eyes and threw my head back.

"So, Jimmy boy," Joe began, "you've been with us a year now – only nineteen more to go."

"Yeah," Biju chimed in, "and when you reach your twenty Joey will still be your driver on the crew."

"Who are you kidding," Joe shot back. "You'll still be tossing cans when Jimmy hits twenty."

Biju shook his head. "Not me. I'm going back to India someday where I'll live like a king."

"Yeah," Joe snickered, "you'll be a king who worships cows."

"Hey," Biju said, "who said Jimmy's gonna leave at twenty. He's probably gonna be a lifer like us."

"Is that true, Jimmy?" Joe asked. "Is tossing garbage cans your lifelong dream?"

I waited a moment for the laughter to subside before I answered. "Actually, my dream was to be a cop."

"Really?" Biju replied. "What happened?"

"These," I said as I tapped the right lens of my glasses with my right index finger. "I couldn't pass the vision test for the cops."

"That's tough," Biju sighed. A grin appeared on his face. "But at least it gave you the opportunity to throw garbage cans."

"Why don't you put in to be a sanitation cop," Joe suggested.

"A what?" I replied.

"A sanitation cop," Biju echoed. "Don't tell me you didn't know we have our own police department."

"I won't tell you," I shrugged, "but it's true. I had no idea there was a Sanitation Police Department."

"How could you not have ever seen our cops riding around in their little Cushman scooters writing summonses for littering and dirty sidewalks?"

"Give the kid a break," Joe said. "He's probably seen them a million times, but they are almost identical to city cops. They wear the same uniform, and the shield looks the same. They carry guns and even the patch looks the same until you look closely and see that it says 'Sanitation Police.'"

"Do you have to take a test?" I asked.

"Nope," Joe replied. "You just apply and get appointed."

"How many sanitation cops are there?" I asked.

"I'm not certain," Joe replied, "but I think there's about 120 cops with the department."

"That's all?" I screeched. "With about nine thousand uniformed members of this department that doesn't sound like great odds."

"You'd be surprised," Joe said. "Not many sanmen want to be cops. They're perfectly content working behind the truck."

"That's right," Biju joined in, "and the opportunity for overtime is much better working the trucks."

"So, you see," Joe continued, "you might very well have a good chance to get on with the sanitation cops."

I threw my arms out to the side. "Nobody ever mentioned the sanitation police during training. I don't even know how to apply."

"Come with me," Joe said.

"Where are we going?" I asked.

"To those payphones on the corner," Joe replied. "I'm gonna call Charlie Malloy."

"Who's Charlie Malloy?"

"Me and Charlie came on the job together. He's in charge of the Sanitation Police Department. I think they call him an inspector."

"What do you mean 'they call him an inspector.' Wouldn't that be his title?"

Joe grabbed the phone. "His title is Sanitation Man. All the cops, no matter what their titles are with the police department have the civil service title of Sanitation Man, unless they were promoted to Foreman."

I stroked my chin. "So, if your friend Charlie left the police, he would..."

"That's right," Joe jumped in, "he'd be behind a truck tossing cans.

Joe held up his hand in the universal stop sign and spoke into the phone. "Hey, Charlie, how's it going? How's the wife and kids? Same old thing with me. We're just waiting for that first grandkid to arrive. Look, Charlie, I'm calling you on a little bit of business. I just found out that the kid whose been on my crew for the past year wanted to be a cop, but he failed the NYPD vision test. I was hoping you could talk to him about the job. That's great. It's our day off tomorrow so I'm sure he can stop by. His name is Jimmy Murphy and he'll be there at ten o'clock sharp. Thanks buddy."

Joe hung up the phone and smiled. "See, Uncle Joe is looking out for you. You have an appointment to meet Inspector Malloy tomorrow morning."

"Where?" I asked.

"Right in your neck of the woods. Do you know where the incinerator and Central Repair Shop is on 58th Street?"

"Sure," I said, "It can't be much more than three miles from where I live in Jackson Heights."

"The Sanitation Police have their central office inside the Central Repair Shop," Joe explained. "Don't make me look bad. Be there on time."

CHAPTER 3:

I had never been inside the Central Repair Shop even though I had passed by it many times. Along with the adjacent incinerator and district garage it sat like an island in Woodside, Queens surrounded by Calvary cemetery to the east and west, and the Brooklyn Queens Expressway and the Long Island Expressway to the north and south. An instructor talked about the Central Repair Shop during training. It made an impression on me when he said the department's fleet of thousands of vehicles were repaired and refurbished in a one million square foot building in Queens, a building that is as long as the Chrysler Building is tall.

I walked up the steep ramp that led to the two huge garage type doors. No one checked my identification when I walked through the door adjacent to the garage doors and entered what looked to be the largest auto mechanics shop in the world. An open lane for vehicle movement ran throughout the entire floor with various machine shops, engine rooms, rebuilding centers, truck repair stations, and fabricating departments lining both sides of the lane.

The nearest person to me was a mechanic who was standing under a superintendent's car that was up on a lift.

"Excuse me," I yelled to be heard over the drone of engines and machinery, "can you tell me where the Sanitation Police office is?"

The mechanic pointed with a wrench toward a stairwell in the corner of the building. Since the building was a two-floor structure, I assumed the police were on the second floor.

I was beginning to breath heavily after covering almost every inch of the office space on the second floor. Finally, in the northeast corner of building, the only area I had not yet checked, I saw a glass door with a large sticker of a Sanitation Police patch adorning the top section of the door.

I looked at my watch and grit my teeth in disgust. It was 10:07. I thought I was going to be early for the appointment but after finding a parking space, getting directed to the second floor, and walking close to a mile through the maze of administrative offices, I was now late. I knocked on the door and waited.

"Come in, it's open," replied the friendly voice.

The office was a complete contradiction the building it occupied. The Central Repair Shop was massive, but this little office stuffed away in one of its corners could not have been more than ten feet by ten feet at most. There was just enough room for a desk, some filing cabinets and two chairs for guests.

The man behind the desk pointed to the chairs in front of his desk. "Come in and make yourself comfortable," he said.

"I'm sorry I'm late," I apologized as I slid into a chair.

"No big deal," the man replied. "Finding this little office up here can be like finding a needle in a haystack. Sometimes I still get lost," he laughed.

When he stood to shake hands, I could see that the man was tall, probably about 6-feet 2-inches. He looked to be in his late fifties and sported a thick head of snow-white hair which looked like he had forgotten to brush this morning. His arms and legs were those of a thin man, but it was apparent that as he advanced through middle age his stomach and torso were not remaining as slim as his limbs.

"I'm Inspector Malloy," he greeted. "So, you're on Joe Recupero's crew."

"I am," I nodded, "and it's a pleasure to meet you too, sir."

Inspector Malloy was dressed in a rumpled white shirt with a dark blue tie. A badge holder displayed an inspectors shield on the shirt pocket. It was the same type of shield NYPD inspectors wore.

Charlie Malloy leaned back in his chair. "So, you're interested in becoming a Sanitation Police Officer."

"Yes, I am, sir."

"Joe told me you failed the NYPD vision test," Malloy said.

"That's correct, sir."

"Is your vision corrected to 20/20?" Malloy asked.

"It is," I replied. "It's 20/70 uncorrected and 20/20 corrected."

"Well," Malloy began, "you meet the vision requirement for our police department." He shook his head. "I always believed that the NYPD's vision requirement was near sighted."

There was a moment of uncomfortable silence until Malloy burst out laughing. "That's a joke, son."

"Oh yeah, that's very funny," I stammered with fake laughter.

Inspector Malloy slapped both hands on his desktop. "Well, I guess I should begin by telling you something about the Sanitation Police Department." He cleared his throat. "The Sanitation Police Department came into existence in 1936, and we are unquestionably the least known force among the city's many law enforcement agencies. We are a group of armed officers whose focus is not drug dealers or murderers but the 30,000 tons of garbage that New Yorkers produce each day."

"There are 122 of us right now," Malloy said, "and most of our work is mundane, like summonsing litterers, catching illegal dumpers and nabbing the dog owner who does not clean up after his pet. Sanitation police officers undergo a six-week training academy at Floyd Bennett Field, the same place you went through your initial training."

"Do you look for anything special in selecting a police officer?" I asked.

"Sanitation Police Officers bring many different experiences to the job, but what they have in common is that they all come from the sanman ranks and have hauled trash and driven trucks, sweepers and snowplows."

"What are the specific qualifications?" I asked.

"Sanmen can apply to the police force after two years on the job and must have a strong record as sanitation workers to be chosen." Malloy said.

My body deflated a bit. "I have just over a year on the job."

"Well," Malloy shrugged, "You can fill out the application and leave it with me. You never know what the future will bring, and in the worst-case scenario, I'll look you up in a year."

...

I tried to place the Sanitation Police out of my mind since it would be almost a year before I could even be considered for the position.

The world is full of insightful sayings. One is, "timing is everything." Another is, "one man's misfortune is another man's fortune." Both of these quotations applied to me when I found a phone message waiting when I returned home from work two weeks after my meeting with Inspector Malloy.

My dad's scribble seemed to read, "Call Mr. Mallory - urgent," followed by a partially legible phone number. I had no idea who Mr. Mallory was, but since it was urgent, I wasted no time in dialing what I hoped was the correct phone number.

I nearly fell over the kitchen table when I heard a voice on the other end of the phone. "Inspector Malloy, may I help you?"

I couldn't catch my breath for a moment, but I was finally able to stutter, "This is James Murphy, sir, returning your call."

"Thanks for getting back to me so promptly, Jim," Malloy said. "I have a big problem that I need your help with, and I have to work fast."

"What can I do to help?" I asked.

"It will come out in the papers tomorrow, but an hour ago the commissioner dismantled virtually the entire police department."

"What?" I gasped.

"That's right," Malloy said. "He held a press conference where he accused our police department of corruption and inefficiency in the enforcement of New York City's sanitation laws, and as a result he demoted all 17 lieutenants and sergeants in the department and about half of the police officers."

"What were they demoted to?" I asked.

"Remember," Malloy began, "everyone in the police department, including me, is actually a sanitation man detailed to an assignment with the police department. All the demoted personnel, regardless of rank were transferred back to work on the garbage trucks."

"How can the police department function without supervisors?" I asked.

"They will be replaced by departmental foremen dressed in their normal sanitation uniforms until new lieutenants and sergeants can be appointed," Malloy explained.

"What caused this?" I asked.

"The commissioner said in his press conference that the shakeup grew out of investigations that found patrolmen were falsifying summonses to cover up malingering, and that the lieutenants and sergeants were just as responsible for allowing the malingering to take place." Malloy took a deep breath and sighed. "Evidently, the investigation has been going on for several months and there have now been disciplinary charges filed against six sanitation patrolmen found to have deliberately falsified summonses to cover up malingering on their posts, with more charges to follow. Three have already pled guilty. One was suspended for 30 days without pay, a second fined $2,100 and a third fined $1,400. The trials of the three other patrolmen and anyone else charged are still pending."

"At least no one lost their job." I remarked.

"People already have lost their jobs," Malloy groaned.

"I don't understand."

"This press conference today," Malloy explained, "was just the straw that broke the camel's back. Last month a patrolman was dismissed after a departmental trial found that he had solicited $50, and later

$100, from an apartment-house manager whom he had been ticketing repeatedly for violations."

"That's not good," I said.

"No, it's not," Malloy agreed, "and that wasn't all. It was like a perfect storm when the investigation found out through a city councilwoman that several of her constituents in Chelsea and Greenwich Village were being harassed by sanitation police through being barraged by summonses for very minor violations like having dented lids on their garbage cans," he said.

"And the commissioner is blaming the sergeants and lieutenants for all of this?" I questioned.

"I've been taking calls all day from sergeants and lieutenants – stand up guys I've known for years. They don't understand why they're being demoted." Malloy continued, "They believe, and frankly, I agree, that the evidence of corruption and malingering were merely signs of a few bad apples." I could hear the inspector gulp before he continued. "Tommy Hughs has been a lieutenant for fifteen years and he has been with the department for 25-years. They don't come any better than Tommy. He is supposed to be getting an award from the mayor next month for catching three armed robbers who beat up an 80-year-old hot dog vendor. How is it going to look when Tommy steps up wearing a sanman uniform and carrying a city litter basket."

"That's a shame," I said.

"Make no mistake," Malloy said, "the timing of this is not coincidental."

"What do you mean?"

"The commissioner also announced the formation of a new branch of the sanitation police. A new enforcement squad of 60 lower-paid sanitation enforcement agents will be hired tomorrow."

"Sixty more cops?" I gasped.

"No," Malloy replied. "These will be civilian agents, like the meter maids who write parking tickets. I believe the commissioner would love to get rid of us altogether, but he knows that armed sanitation police sometimes perform duties, such as confronting the drivers of trucks that were dumping illegally, that are too risky for ticketing agents."

"Are you okay, sir?" I inquired.

"I guess so," Malloy replied. "Actually, I'm in charge of the department now."

"Congratulations," I offered.

"There's nothing really to be congratulated for," he said. "Someone had to run the department, and I'm just the last man standing. If my name comes up in this investigation tomorrow, I'll be behind a truck tossing cans too."

"How can I help, sir?" I repeated my earlier offer.

"I need for you to agree to come on board as a police officer."

"What about the two-year requirement?" I asked.

"Screw the two-year requirement," Malloy blurted. I have to fill the ranks of the department with at least forty new police officers by next week so we can start a class and get them out in the field in six weeks." Malloy hesitated for a moment before continuing. "I'm sorry to be so blunt, James, but I have a lot of calls to make. Are you in?"

"Yeah, yeah," I stammered, "I'm in."

"Thanks," Malloy replied. "When you go back to work the orders detailing you to the police department will be at your district, but I can tell you now, you'll be reporting to Floyd Bennett Field to begin training next Monday."

"Thank you for the opportunity, sir," I said.

"Thanks for helping out and welcome aboard." The click indicated the call had been ended before I could even consider another response. It took me several minutes to digest what had just transpired. Forty minutes later as I lounged on the living room sofa sipping a soda and munching on Oreo cookies watching Love Connection on TV, it finally hit me. It may not be the NYPD, but next Monday I was going to become a cop in New York City.

I didn't tell my friends about my upcoming journey into the world of law enforcement. I was spending less time at the Swagman and Kate Cassidy's because more and more I had become detached from my police officer friends, a fact that Kevin seemed to relish every time we got together. There was a bright side to my situation. I was not spending nearly as much money as I usually would at the bars, and since I could not get into the Galacta arcade game, I wasn't throwing away rolls of quarters like I used to when the Space Invaders game was in the Swagman.

My old man was pragmatic, if not supportive. He shrugged and said it was okay to become a sanitation cop as long as I maintained my civil service title of sanitation man. The roughest part of my impending assignment was saying goodbye to Joe and Biju. I admit to shedding a few tears when we hugged and parted company after my last day on the route.

CHAPTER 4:

It was déjà vu being back on that tarmac at Floyd Bennett Field, but very quickly the similarities between the training I had gone through a year earlier and the police training I was about to begin became apparent. First of all, there were less trainees on the tarmac than a year ago. Inspector Malloy had apparently accomplished his goal as I counted forty men milling around, waiting to begin police training. The appearance of the instructors revealed this training experience was going to be much different that basic sanman school. Instead of the affable, fatherly attitude displayed by most of the instructors during sanman training, the military atmosphere with instructors shouting like drill instructors began immediately. The screaming was a shock to the system, but I got accustomed to it quickly. Some trainees could not get used to it and two men on that first day had a few choice words for the instructors before quitting to go back to working behind the trucks. As the two men walked off the property, the lead instructor stood in front of the entire group that was standing motionless at attention and snarled, "Anyone else?" No one moved. Police training had begun.

The lead instructor identified himself as Police Officer Smith. He did not say how long he had been a sanman, but he said he had been with the training academy for eight years, and that he had served four years in the Marine Corp. Officer Smith looked like a Marine. He was tall and solidly lean with a high and tight crew cut. He had one of those faces that was hard to stamp an age on. He was probably in his mid-thirties, but I would not have been shocked to learn he was fifty.

Smith got right to the point once we were all seated inside a trailer classroom. "Wearing this uniform out on the street, you must be trained for the unexpected. You men will wear the same uniforms and bulletproof vests and carry the same guns that New York City police officers do. The only distinguishing feature is your shoulder patch that reads Sanitation Police." His eyes widened and his nostril flared as he glared at the class. "You better be damn proud of that patch."

The next six weeks flew by. The training was great, but I was a little disappointed to learn that I wasn't really a police officer. My job title was police officer but as far as New York State legal authority was concerned, I took an oath as a New York State peace officer. Police officers and peace officers are sworn law enforcement officers, and although there are some subtle differences, both carry firearms, make arrests, and issue summonses. That was enough for me.

As far as I could tell, we were being trained much like other city police officers, only during a more condensed time period with more specialized topics. The instructors emphasized safety and told us always be on the lookout for confrontations that could suddenly turn violent. During one class out on the tarmac, the potential danger of confronting violators was not lost on the recruits, even as we tried to stifle laughs as instructors acted out the stopping of a driver in traffic.

"You pulled me over for littering?" shouted Police Officer John Velez, the instructor playing the sanitation scofflaw who had just lobbed a drink container out his car window. "What are you bothering me for?" he continued with escalating attitude. "Why don't you go arrest a drug dealer or something?"

But the 38 fresh-faced recruits, including myself, turned somber when another instructor, Police Officer William Green, showed us the finer points of frisking a suspect and told us how to stand to avoid getting shot. He stressed that pulling a car over, even for something as seemingly innocuous as littering, could turn into a life-threatening situation.

Green said that once on the street, most sanitation police officers patrol alone, and that most of the work involved tickets to store owners who had neglected to sweep their sidewalks or clean the gutters in front of their businesses, and tickets to homeowners and apartment building managers for not keeping their sidewalks clean. But he also noted that there were special units to investigate illegal dumping and hazardous waste problems.

I became friendly with Hector Santiago, a 24-year-old recruit who sat next to me in the trailer. Hector had been a sanman for three years and said he was happy to be trading in his garbage- hauling tasks for police work.

"I've already heard all the wisecracks from my friends," he chuckled, "like: 'hey, you're a garbage cop, come and protect my garbage.'"

My thoughts immediately flashed to Kevin. "I know exactly what you mean, brother."

"But I don't pay much attention to it," Hector continued, "because no matter what they say, this is important work."

Important work – in my quest to obtain a badge and gun I had never stopped to consider if the work was important. I was going to have to think about that for a while.

Whether the work was important or not, the instructors stressed how the work could be dangerous. They highlighted that the more perilous duties involved having to stake out vacant lots to catch illegal dumpers or put on protective gear to investigate the criminal disposal of asbestos or toxic wastes. Instructor Smith would constantly remind us that as highly visible uniformed officers on the street with a legal duty to act, we could also become involved with everything the NYPD handles, including domestic disputes, shootings and stabbings.

The only time we left Floyd Bennett Field was to spend a week at a private firearms range on the West Side of Manhattan, learning the safe handling and functioning of a 4-inch Smith & Wesson Model 10 revolver. I was quite proud of myself when I qualified as a pistol expert at the end of the week.

On graduation day, my dad hugged me, and my mom wept and said how proud she was, just like my previous graduation, but this time I was wearing the dress blue uniform of a police officer – a Sanitation Police Officer.

The sanitation commissioner made a speech in which he talked about how essential the Sanitation Police Department was to the safety of the city and the role of the department. I found that a bit odd since six weeks earlier he had demoted most of the personnel in the department.

When I walked up to the makeshift stage set up outside one of the trailers, I shook hands with the commissioner and saluted Inspector Malloy, who winked and smiled as he handed my diploma to me.

For me, the highlight of the day came at the very end of the ceremony. Instructor Smith shouted, "Academy, dismissed!" We all cheered and tossed our hats in the air and then gravitated to our family and friends. After receiving well wishes from my parents I received a tap on the shoulder. I turned to see the smiling faces of Joe and Biju.

"Oh my God!" I sang as I hugged them both. "Thanks so much for coming."

"It's no big deal," Joe said.

"yeah" Biju followed up. "It's our day off and we had nothing else better to do."

To me, the presence of my two former partners was the best way to end the day.

CHAPTER 5:

The graduates received the next two days off, and on the third day I was excited to begin my police career. I was assigned to report to the district 11 garage in Brooklyn on Shore Parkway at 6 A.M. The police department had two trailers set up outside the garage. One trailer was a locker room for the cops and the other was an administrative office. After getting into uniform, I entered the administrative trailer and sat in one of the school-style metal folding chairs with desktops that were set up in three rows. At six o'clock eight cops were occupying the chairs, three of whom were part of my graduating class.

There was a smaller office inside the trailer and from behind the door to that office emerged a uniformed sanitation foreman in his distinctive green uniform. He held a clipboard in his hand and made no eye contact with the seated cops as he called the roll and gave out the assignments for the day. I was assigned special post 1. I was excited at the prospect of working something special on my first day on patrol, and my excitement only grew when the foreman told me to hang around after roll call because I would be going out with him.

The foreman drove the dark blue sedan with the official New York City plates through the streets of Brooklyn as he explained my special assignment.

"Do you know where Lombardy Street is?" he asked.

I shook my head. "No."

"Well," he chuckled, "by the end of the day you'll know it well."

"What's going on there?" I asked.

"Lombardy Street is an industrial area that dead ends at Newtown Creek. We've been getting numerous complaints from the community and the local politicians of illegal dumping on the street."

"Why do people dump there?" I asked.

"Because it's easy," the foreman replied. "They dump everything there – crates, barrels, giant bags of food, household trash. We don't have the manpower right now to run a plainclothes operation and make arrests while they're in the act of dumping, but the next best thing we can do is put a uniform out there to deter the dumping."

When the sedan made a right turn 35-minutes later I saw 'Lombardy Street' on the sign at the corner. As the foreman drove down an exceptionally long block towards a dead end I saw nothing but auto salvage yards, several auto glass shops, a trucking company, some auto body shops, and a bunch of seemingly abandoned buildings lining the street. The foreman made a U-turn at the dead-end sign and stopped the car. "Okay," he said, "this is your post."

"What do I do here?" I asked.

"Just walk up and down the block and make sure no one dumps any garbage."

"What if I need help? Don't we have radios?"

"Not today," he replied. "Some of the police radios are out for repair and there weren't enough to go around today."

The foreman pointed way down to the next corner. "There's a payphone down there. If it works, you can use it to call 911."

"And if it doesn't work?"

"Most of these businesses are open," he said. "Ask one of them to use the phone." The foreman continued with a different topic. "You might want to find out what businesses are open anyway so you can use a bathroom."

"What if I can't find an open business?" I moaned.

The foreman shrugged. "I don't know what to tell you, kid. Go to the bathroom in the weeds, there's plenty of them on the block."

"You want me to go to the bathroom in the street?" I blurted.

"Only number one," the foreman clarified. "Don't go number two in the street unless it's a real emergency."

"Of course not," I scoffed.

"You're entitled to an hour meal," the foreman continued, "and on a post like this you can take it whenever you want."

I was out of the car now and I extended my arms to the side. "Where am I gonna go for meal?"

"I don't know kid. You have to improvise." He pointed to a milk crate on the sidewalk among some high weeds. "You can sit on that crate during your meal. At least you'll take a load off your feet."

"Gee, thanks," I said.

"Someone will be out here to pick you up later," he said as he began to drive off.

"When?" I called out to the moving car.

The foreman stopped momentarily and hung his head out the window. "As soon as we can find someone to relieve you on the next tour. Have a good day."

I watched the car get smaller as it rolled down the long block and then disappear when it made a left turn. I thought back to my classmate Hector's remark about the sanitation police doing important work. I'd have to remember that when I was taking a leak on the sidewalk later. And then I took a deep breath and began to walk.

For the next four hours I walked back and forth on the very long dirty industrial dead-end street. The sound of my footsteps echoed of the walls of the buildings and factories that may or may not have been abandoned. The street was littered with trash, broken glass, and rusty metal scraps. I took care with my steps, avoiding the debris as best I could. I wished the foreman was still here so I could tell him it was too late to prevent any dumping. In fact, someone could dump a truck load of garbage on the block, and I doubt I would notice the difference. On one area of the block the smell was overpowering, a combination of burnt rubber, diesel fumes, and stagnant water. The air was thick and oppressive, making it hard to breath. The buildings on either side of the street were different sizes and shapes, but most were in disrepair with their brick facades stained and cracked. Many windows were broken, and I saw some doors hanging off their hinges.

When I would come to the dead end I would rest for a few minutes and stare out to the filthy polluted waters of Newtown Creek. The first time I reached the other end of the block where the foreman had turned, I noted that the intersecting road was Varick Street. I grabbed the payphone on the southeast corner and put it up to my ear – dead. I looked both ways on Varick Street and did not see any signs of a place where I could eat, rest, or relieve myself. I made a few more laps on Lombardy Street and saw very few signs of life. Every now and then a car or truck would roll down the block and enter a building through a roll up garage door that would quickly close as soon as the vehicle was inside. I figured no one would come out of any of these buildings to offer me a glass of lemonade on this hot day. Afterall, junk yards and body shops with their reputation for questionable legal ethics would not be thrilled to see a uniformed cop pacing around outside their sites.

By noon, I figured I had walked over six miles. I considered myself to be in good physical condition, but every part of my body was aching. I could even feel my hair tingling with pain. What I had considered a joke when the foreman had dropped me off had become reality. I staggered to the milk crate on the sidewalk among the high weeds and sat down. It felt better than my old man's easy chair in our living room. I was probably on the verge of dehydration, but at least I had not had the urge to urinate because another stark reality was setting in. If I did have to take a leak, I was going to take care of my business right there in the weeds. It wouldn't be these weeds, however. I may still want to sit on the milk crate and unlike my dog, I don't think I would enjoy the smell of my nearby urine.

At least six times I intended to rise off the milk crate and six times I stopped. It wasn't that I couldn't get up – at least I think it wasn't. Every time my butt began to rise from the crate my mind seemed to push me back down and say, "stay there, you idiot. No one is watching you."

That thought made sense to me as I stayed planted on the crate. Further down the block tons of garbage could have been in the process of being dumped and I wouldn't have known about it, nor would I have cared.

A semblance of a breeze had picked up, ruffling the weeds and giving me a smidgen of relief. It was enough of a peaceful, pleasant feeling that it forced my eyes to involuntarily close. I never perceived the car pulling up to the curb next to me.

"Who the hell are you?"

I awoke from my brief slumber to see that the inquiry had come from the open passenger window of a car, and not just any car. I quickly stood to approach the NYPD patrol car that had pulled up next to my weeds.

"This is my post," I sheepishly said.

"Wow!" the cop chuckled. "Who did you piss off?"

The cop and his partner shared a laugh before I continued. "This is my first day on patrol and I'm supposed to be preventing dumping on the block."

"Jesus!" the cop shook his head, "with all the shit on this block who the hell would know if anything more was dumped?"

The driver lowered his head to make eye contact with me out of the passenger window. "What are you doing sitting in the weeds?" he grinned.

"I was taking a break," I said. "It's the only place out here I could find."

"Unbelievable," he scoffed. "Jump in the back, kid. We're going 63 back at the house. You can come with us."

During training we had had a brief class on 10-codes, so I was reasonably sure that "63" was short for 10-63, which was the code for meal period. I was also certain that "house" was their precinct, but at this point they could have been going to any house and it would not have mattered. The back seat of 0-pthe patrol car with its ripped upholstery felt heavenly, even better than the milk crate.

The house turned out to be the 94th Precinct on Meserole Street, about a mile away from my post. After a pit stop at a local pizza joint, I sat in the precinct lounge eating a slice and slurping down a refreshing cold soda with my two new friends.

Don Sutton and Mike Grimaldi reminded me very much of Joe and Biju. They were both veterans with many years on the job and both were affable fellows who were understanding of the plight of this rookie out on his first day of patrol. Most of all, they weren't talking down to me. There was no attempt to humiliate me like Kevin would have when they had found me in a completely humiliating circumstance.

When they dropped me off back on Lombardy Street they didn't leave immediately. They were shocked when they found out that I did not have a radio, so they were going to look out for me for the rest of the tour.

"This is our sector, Jim," Mike said, "so if we don't get tied up on jobs we'll drive by and check on you every hour or so."

"Thanks," I nodded.

"We can't have you sitting in the weeds anymore," Don laughed. He hit the siren on the patrol car several times until a man stuck his head out of a steel door next to a closed rollup garage door. "Come out here, Angelo," Don bellowed.

A very large, round swarthy man wearing a work shirt and pants covered in grease and oil cautiously approached the patrol car.

"Don't worry," Don said. "There's no problem. Officer Murphy is assigned to the block to prevent illegal dumping."

Angelo seemed instantly to be more at ease. "That's good," he nodded. "There's too much of that dumping shit going on here. The block looks like a shithole."

"I want you to let Officer Murphy use your bathroom and phone if he needs it."

"No problem," Angelo replied. He pointed to the steel door. "Just ring the bell and I'll let you right in."

"Thanks," I said.

I heard static from the radio inside the car and Don talking into the microphone. "We gotta go on a job, "Mike said, "we'll see you later."

"Thanks for everything, guys," I said.

As I watched the patrol car turn right on Varick Street I realized everything had changed. Yes, I was still on the same lousy post, and yes, I would have to walk for at least another four hours until hopefully being picked up, and yes, the heat was still stifling. But my encounter with Don and Mike changed everything. Before they rolled up on my weeds, I was considering going back to the police trailer and turning in my badge and gun to go back behind a garbage truck, but Don and Mike had made me feel different. They made me feel like a cop.

CHAPTER 6:

The rest of the summer consisted of a potpourri of unique "police" assignments. Due to a newspaper story about the misuse of fire hydrants in the city by youngsters who would illegally open them to spray passing vehicles, I was detailed for three consecutive days to stand by a fire hydrant in a residential Brooklyn neighborhood where the most complaints been reported.

On another occasion I was detailed to work with my old academy classmate Hector, who had made the statement about sanitation police work being important. On this day our important work was to accompany the Sanitation Commissioner on a walking tour of the area around Washington Square Park so he could play no-nonsense tough guy clean city crusader while he ordered me and Hector to write summonses to people he observed littering and businesses with dirty sidewalks. It goes without saying that this was the most undesirable of my special assignments and it took all of our communication skills to talk irate pedestrians and store owners from attempting to strangle the commissioner. I recall when we were dismissed from our detail with the commissioner I turned to Hector and said, "that was real important work, wasn't it?"

He shrugged and said, "Of course it was. We kept the commissioner from getting killed."

The best assignment, and I mean that sarcastically, I received that summer was just as some of the crispness of the fall was beginning to push away New York City's stifling summer heat. Approximately a year earlier the mayor had signed into law a bill making the owner, leasee, tenant, occupant, or person in charge of any building or premises responsible for cleaning the street 18-inches from the curb in front of their homes or businesses.

In theory, the law made sense. A major reason street dirt built up was because when homeowners and merchants swept their sidewalks

– as they are supposed to do – they often pushed the sweepings into the gutter and didn't pick them up. Since the Sanitation Department, like all other city agencies was still getting back on its feet since the layoffs of the mid 70s, street sweeping was not as frequent as it used to be, and the dirt and trash would sometimes remain next to the curb for days. The new law also provided a remedy to the bad habits of private sanitation collections. In too many cases, merchants would improperly package their refuse when they placed it at the curbside for nighttime collection. When the private carters arrived, some of this material would often spill into the street as a result of the poor packaging and was not picked up by the private carter, as it should have been. This clean gutter law now placed the responsibility on the merchant to clean up any spilled material or face a summons with a hefty fine. The Sanitation Commissioner said that even though the law had been in place for a year, enforcement had been delayed because he wanted to give New Yorkers a fair chance to adjust to the new law before the summons barrage began.

That was the theory. The reality was me being chased down a Chinatown street by two elderly Asian women wielding broomsticks after I tried to issue them a summons for the dirty curb in front of their restaurant. It certainly was embarrassing, but I firmly believed discretion was the better part of valor in that case. I did not want to have to justify shooting two elderly women over a dirty sidewalk.

I had one more assignment that ranked right up there with my brush with combat with the elderly women. During the first week of October, I was assigned to posts in Queens to patrol commercial business areas that had numerous complaints for having dirty sidewalks. My first post was in the neighborhood of Corona. Specifically, I was to patrol a stretch of 103rd Street near the elevated subway station. The subway was not just a landmark for me, because with no vehicles available, I had to take the train from the police trailer in Brooklyn out to my post in Queens. Even though roll call at the trailer had been at 6 A.M., it was just before eight o'clock that I carefully navigating down the steps of the elevated 103rd Street subway station.

The sidewalk teemed with people as I strolled past the Chinese produce market, the Argentine restaurant, the Mexican bakery, and the sneaker outlet. Jackson Heights was not that far away from Corona, but I could never remember actually being on 103rd Street before. Despite the crowded conditions on this heavily trafficked street, I was amazed at how clean the sidewalk was. I shook my head with the realization that there wouldn't be much business for me here. And then, I saw it – a very worn looking yellow awning that contained the simple red letters spelling out VARIETY STORE. The awning and sign were not what really caught my attention. What I was focused on was the filthy condition of the sidewalk and curb in front of the store. The sidewalk appeared to be the world's fair of garbage with trash and litter from all over the globe occupying spaces on the sidewalk. There were newspapers with print in several different languages along with banana peels, partially eaten pineapples and tacos, not to mention your run of the mill dirt and paper.

I entered the store, and my focus was immediately drawn to the left where I observed what might have been the largest collection of pornographic magazines covering the entire wall. A middle eastern man in his twenties was behind the counter to the right transacting the sale of several pornographic magazines to a greasy looking obese man. The clerk did not acknowledge my presence, but a middle aged middle eastern male came out from a door at the back of the store and came directly to me.

"What do you want?" he sneered.

"Your sidewalk is filthy," I said.

"So?" the man shrugged.

"So, I'm going to give you a summons for the dirty sidewalk, and I want you to clean it."

The greasy fat man departed with his stash of porno magazines in a plain brown bag, freeing the clerk to become involved with my visit. The two men began a very animated conversation among themselves in Arabic while I wrote the summons. I had no idea what they were saying, but by the tone I was sure they weren't commenting on what a good job I was doing.

Suddenly the younger man called out to me. "Hey cop," he said in strained English, "You racist – you against Iran."

I ignored the comment and finished writing the summons. Tensions were strained with Iran. It had not been that long ago that the American hostages who were held in Iran for 444 days were finally released. Maybe the man was right. Like many Americans I was not a big fan of Iran at that time. The funny thing was, however, I didn't realize these men were Iranian until he made the comment.

The summons I wrote was called an ECB summons because it was returnable to the Environmental Control Board. I tore out the pink copy of the summons and handed it to the older man. Normally, I would have explained all the options for paying or fighting the summons in great detail but for these two creeps I simply said, "All the information is on the back of the summons."

I read a lot of comic books as a kid, and I still dabbled in them as an adult, so my "Spidey Sense" was tingling when I got out to the sidewalk. I turned quickly to see that the two men had followed me outside. The older man still held the pink summons in his hand and appeared to be surveying the big job he would have cleaning his sidewalk. The younger man snatched the summons from his partner's hand and yelled, "Hey, cop!" He then tore the summons into four pieces, and spit on the torn pieces before throwing the summons to join the rest of the trash on the sidewalk. I remained very calm while the older man pulled his wild-eyed compatriot back inside the store. I leaned against a parked car and wrote two more summonses – one for littering and the other for spitting. I re-entered the store and calmly handed the two pink copies to the older male. I nodded toward the younger man and said, "If he wants to try anything stupid – let him try. I'll drag both your asses to jail."

I backed out of the store and kept my eyes on the door until I was across the street. Even on the other side of the street I could still hear the men screaming in Arabic. That was the only day I was assigned to 103rd Street, but I made a promise to myself that if I ever was assigned to patrol the area again, I would give special attention to that variety store.

Despite the less than stellar summer assignments with my near thrashing at the hands of the old Chinese ladies, and the international incident I almost incited in Corona, I had actually become accustomed to the job, and it may sound strange, but I was beginning to like it. What was most bizarre what that I still found that most of my good feelings for the job could be traced back to that first day on patrol and how good my friends from the 94th precinct, Don and Mike, had made me feel.

•••

Whatever the reason, life was good. I was spending more time with my friends, and I wasn't letting Kevin's verbal barbs bother me, no matter how hard he tried – and he did try.

Kevin was spending his bar time exclusively at Kate Cassidy's with his cop buddies and groupies, and every time I entered, I could always count on a verbal onslaught. On one particular night a group of nurses from St. John's hospital were celebrating a co-worker's birthday, so with an audience of mostly single young ladies present, Kevin was in rare form. He spewed everything from, "He's not a real cop – he's a garbage cop," to "He's got to go handle an emergency – someone just littered outside."

Maybe I had become numb to his incessant verbal jabs, but the insults didn't bother me as much anymore. In fact, even though I didn't realize it at the moment, one of the shots he took at me that I did not hear was to have a profound impact on the rest of my life.

Kevin seemed to be taking a break before beginning the next round of assault on me. In the meantime, I sat at the bar nursing my beer and watching the Yankees beat the Orioles on the small TV mounted on the wall. The stool on my left was empty, but with my "Spidey Sense" always turned on, I sensed someone moving onto the stool, but I kept my focus on the ballgame. The between inning commercials were running as I heard a strange sound to my left. It was a "sniffing" sound. I ignored it at first, but when it became more intense, I spun quickly on the stool to observe a strange sight. A very cute blonde, who I assumed was one of the nurses, was extending her head close to my shoulder, and she appeared to be sniffing me.

I reflexively recoiled back in the stool. "May I help you?"

"He's wrong," the girl said.

"Who's wrong?" I questioned.

"Your friend," she replied.

I was still clueless. "What friend?"

She pointed to the other side of the square bar where Kevin was holding court.

"Oh, him," I groaned, assuming that a punch line was forthcoming. "What was he wrong about?" I sighed.

"You don't smell like garbage," she laughed.

"That's the nicest thing anyone has said to me in a long time," I replied.

"Well, I'm glad I could bring a little joy to your day," she smiled and extended her hand. "I'm Kristen."

"I'm Jim," I said as I accepted the handshake. I was surprised and thrilled that Kristen was not sliding off the stool to run back to report to Kevin. She was firmly planted on the stool ready to stay with me.

"What are you drinking," I asked.

"White wine."

"I waved to the bartender. "White wine, please, Timmy."

Years later I still get a kick from telling the story of how I met my wife.

CHAPTER 7:

As the weeks passed and my relationship with Kristin blossomed, I was spending more and more time at Kate Cassidy's, which had quickly become our place to hang out. Although my focus at the pub was exclusively on Kristen, I suddenly became aware of something strange. Kevin was gone. It wasn't like he had gradually faded away – he seemed to disappear. He went from being a fixture holding court at the southeast corner of the square bar to being a ghost – a non-existent entity.

One evening I was waiting at the bar for Kristen to get off work when Larry and Billy entered the pub. After a few moments of greetings and small talk, I asked what I thought was an innocent question - boy, was I wrong.

"Where's Kevin been lately?"

Larry and Billy glanced at each other before Larry responded. "You didn't hear?"

"Hear what?" I replied.

"That Kevin turned out to be a fucking rat!" Billy sneered.

"What?" I gasped.

Larry nodded and sighed. "I'm sorry to say he's right."

I held up both my hands in the universal stop sign. "Wait a minute. What exactly are you two talking about?"

"I have a buddy in Internal Affairs who told me the whole story," Larry said.

"Aren't IAB investigations supposed to be confidential?" I asked.

"Of course, they are," Larry replied. "What's your point?"

"Silly me," I snickered. "Sorry, go ahead with the story."

"Okay," Larry began, "so the way I hear it, Kevin's team in Queens Narcotics hit a Bodega in the one-oh-three (police jargon for the 103rd Precinct) and when they took down the door it was a real 'Chinese Fire Drill."

Even with my limited knowledge of NYPD operations, I knew what Larry was talking about. When a search warrant was being executed by a Narcotic team, they could either call the Emergency Service Unit to take down the door, or they could do it themselves. ESU members were professionally trained to make these entries, so they tended to be a little more orderly and by the numbers, while there was much more chance of a frantic "Chinese fire Drill" when Narcotics teams hit a door themselves.

"Why didn't they get ESU to take the door down?" I asked.

"Priorities," Larry replied.

"What does that mean?" I asked.

"ESU's priority when they hit a door is safety," Larry explained. "When the Narco-Rangers make the entry, their priorities are speed and preservation of evidence. While ESU is methodically clearing an apartment room by room, some drug mule is in the rear bathroom flushing all the product down the toilet."

"So, what happened," I asked.

"So, Kevin's team took the door down themselves and within seconds they're running all over the Bodega – upstairs and the basement too,"

"Did they find anything?" I asked.

"Larry smiled. "According to my buddy, Kevin and another Narco-Ranger hit the mother lode in an upstairs closet."

"How much?"

"A half million in cash and four kilos of cocaine."

"What did they do?" I asked.

"They took the prisoners to the one-oh-three and vouchered the money and drugs."

"So, what's the problem?"

Larry sighed. "They vouchered four kilos and $250 thousand."

"Oh," I nodded.

"So, after they finish at the precinct the team goes back to their base. "Do you know where Queens Narcotics is?

I shook my head. "No."

"Queens Narcotics is in a building in the Creedmoor Psychiatric Center, a huge expanse in eastern Queens," Larry explained. "I think it's over 300-acres and has over fifty buildings. The parking lot used by members of Queens Narcotics is almost a quarter mile from the building. It was in that dimly lit parking lot that the team was going to divvy up their score." Larry hesitated and took a deep breath. "There was only one problem."

"What?"

"IAB had a case open on the team and had been watching them for weeks. When the team members gathered around an open trunk to split up the cash, headlights and flashlights from all sides illuminated the open trunk and the men gathered around it. It was IAB."

"What happened then?" I asked.

"Well, "Larry said. "At that point my buddy gave me the story of what specifically happened to Kevin."

"And what was that?"

"Kevin was thrown into the back of a car with an IAB lieutenant, sergeant, and detective and driven to a local hotel."

"What hotel?"

"The Kew Motor Inn," Larry snickered. "It's one of those 'No-tell-motels' where secret lovers can get together covertly for affordable hourly rates."

"Sounds like you could do a commercial for the place." I laughed.

"He probably could," Billy jumped in. "Larry has sampled every room – the Safari room, waterfall room, New York Skyline room."

"Don't forget the Arabian Knights room," Larry corrected.

"Alright, alright," I said impatiently, "What happened?"

"So, they get Kevin in a room," Larry continued, "and the IAB lieutenant looks Kevin square in the eye and says, 'We ain't got you good – we got you perfect. You got one chance and one chance only to make this right. If you don't give it all up right now, next stop will be a precinct cell which will be followed at some point by a nice long stay in a state prison cell.'"

"What did Kevin do?" I asked.

"According to my buddy," Larry said, "Kevin gave it all up immediately."

"Yeah," Billy chimed in, "the fucking rat gave up everything while the rest of the team was hanging tough."

I looked at Larry. "Is that true?"

Larry nodded. "My buddy said Kevin was the only team member to flip. All the others were hanging tough with a story that the money had somehow got separated from the rest of the cash and that they had just become aware of it and were about to return it."

"That's ridiculous," I scoffed.

"Maybe," Larry shrugged, "but it became a moot point when Kevin became a rat."

"Give him a break," I said, "We might have done the same thing under similar circumstances.

Billy waved his index finger vigorously in front of my face. "No, we wouldn't have done the same thing, and you wouldn't have either."

"You're probably right," I said as I changed my focus back to Larry. "So, what happened to Kevin?" I asked.

"He was suspended and after he testifies against all his partners, he'll be fired, but he won't face criminal charges or jail time. The rest of his team is probably going away for a long time."

"Have you guys seen Kevin?" I asked.

"Of course not," Billy snarled, "and that rat knows better than to show his face around here."

"That's pretty cold, isn't it." I remarked.

"Since when did you, of all people, become so benevolent," Billy mocked. "That rat spent the last two years breaking your balls incessantly about being a garbage man and a garbage cop."

I bit my lip. "I know, but this is different."

"A rat is a rat," Billy declared. "that's all I know."

"Hey guys," the familiar voice was joined by a warm hand on my neck.

I spun around on the stool." "Hey babe," I said before planting a kiss on Kristin's lips.

"What's new fellas," Kristin asked.

"Billy shook his head. "Not much."

CHAPTER 8:

I continued to turn out from the trailer in Brooklyn, but I was flying to posts all over the city. The job became somewhat routine as I worked day shifts in an assigned patrol area writing summonses to businesses and homeowners for violating the various sanitation laws. Much as I had become accustomed to Kevin's verbal taunts, I quickly got used to the rants of my summons recipients.

Speaking of Kevin, the trial of his narcotics team was all over the news for a week. Kevin was the prosecution's star witness, and all five defendants were found guilty and received sentences ranging from eight to fifteen years in prison. Kevin was fired from the NYPD, and no one had seen him since. Larry said he heard Kevin was driving a cab in Manhattan, but that was just rumor.

Overall, life was good. I had a wonderful girlfriend, and, in the spring, I was approaching my first anniversary on the job – the police job, that is. Remember, I was still a civil service sanitation man with two years on the job. As the anniversary approached, I received the opportunity to work in plainclothes for a while. Hector was my partner, and we were assigned to work in an unmarked sedan within the 69th Precinct in the Canarsie section of Brooklyn. In the NYPD, plainclothes anti-crime teams were used frequently to battle street crimes like robberies, burglaries, and drug deals. Our assignment was a bit more specialized.

Three years earlier the governor signed a law requiring all pet owners to clean up after their dogs in public places or risk a $100 fine. The law seemed to have been effective in Midtown Manhattan where tourists visiting the big city returned to their homes to tell their friends they only had to take a few dodging steps to cross the street in front of the Plaza Hotel. Those frequenting the Midtown area went as far as to say that the mayor had taken a dirty situation away from the street, put it in a plastic bag, and gotten rid of it. But the mayor hadn't tried walking around the streets in the outer boroughs, particularly areas like Canarsie. Three years after the institution of the pooper scooper law, groups like the I Love a Clean Canarsie Coalition were making noise. They were demanding a crackdown on area residents who did not clean up after their dogs. Apparently, Hector and I were the answer to their prayers.

We would get out to the neighborhood just after sunrise and park around areas where dogwalkers would usually take their pets on a morning stroll. Once fido would do his business and walk away with his owner, leaving his trophy on the curb for all to admire, and step in, we would pounce and issue the dog owner a big, fat $100 summons. The recipients of the summonses weren't happy, and we had more than one dog show his teeth to us, but I was surprised at the support we received from the community. Evidently, there were many residents who were tired of stepping in dog crap.

As much as I enjoyed policing dog poop, Inspector Malloy had different ideas for Hector and me. A change in state law required a temporary redeployment of resources. Under expanded powers granted by the State Legislature, the Sanitation Department mailed out 1,400 final notices to scofflaws who accounted for more than 12,000 outstanding summonses. Hector and I wedged into Inspector Malloy's tiny office to receive our next marching orders.

"The sanitation police will begin serving arrest warrants on building superintendents, landlords, and merchants who are multiple violators of the Health and Administrative Code. The warrant squad of the sanitation police will serve arrest warrants on those who fail to respond to the final notice."

Hector and I looked at each other. "We have a warrant squad?" I asked.

Malloy smiled. "We do now."

"What?" I gasped.

"Congratulations, gentlemen," Malloy nodded, "this is a historical moment for the department – formation of the warrant squad."

"Is this a permanent assignment?" Hector asked.

"Of course not," Malloy scoffed. "You'll execute the warrants and make the arrests. People will get the idea that it's not a good idea to become a sanitation scofflaw and the problem will be solved."

"What about us?" I asked.

"Then I'll find greener pastures for you two," Malloy grinned. "But let's not get ahead of ourselves," the Inspector cautioned. "Let me explain a little bit more about the assignment. According to the city's Environmental Protection Administrator, the worst offenders have accumulated more than 75 summonses. You will begin your work in Brooklyn and then work your way through the other boroughs. The Sanitation Department will use a computerized system to aid in this enforcement program. Eventually, more than 40,000 final notices will be mailed to scofflaws with outstanding summonses dating ten years. You boys will arrest not only those people who have not disposed of their summonses, but also those who fail to appear in court after a trial date has been scheduled and those who have been found guilty but fail to pay their fines. Up to now, the law could be circumvented because violators would simply refuse to appear in court," Malloy said. "Now, we'll be able to issue summonses with some teeth in them."

On day one, the new warrant squad's operations were executed flawlessly. At 6 A.M. we drove our unmarked vehicle to Long Island City, armed with a list of scofflaws in the area. The first victim was the owner of a small coffee shop on Jackson Avenue. The short, rotund, Greek gentleman instantly became cooperative when I explained that he would receive a Desk Appearance Ticket at the precinct, known as a D.A.T., and be back at his coffee shop in a couple of hours. I emphasized that how quick he was back at his business depended in a large part on how cooperative he was. When the desk sergeant at the 108th Precinct issued the man his appearance ticket, we even drove him back to his shop, putting him back in business at 10:30 AM. The shop owner even thanked us as we pulled away from the curb.

I knew that executing arrest warrants couldn't be that easy, but for the remainder of the day, it was. Hector and I found two more scofflaws on our list in Long Island City. In both instances the subjects were business owners who fully cooperated in having their appearance tickets processed at the precinct, and both business owners were back in their stores in two hours.

When Hector and I went off duty we stopped off at the Swagman for a celebratory drink. I had not been in the Swagman for several months, but nothing seemed to have changed. Pete, the owner, was still behind the bar, and his late afternoon "crowd" consisted of a few drunks spread out along the bar silently staring into their drinks. I was disappointed to see that Galacta was still sitting up against the wall opposite the bar.

"Hey, Pete," I greeted, "Give us two cold brews."

"Coming up."

When the two frosty mugs with the perfectly formed heads were in front of us, I raised my beer in a toast. "To sanitation scofflaws – may they all cooperate like our three friends today."

"Here, here," Hector said as our mugs clinked.

The beer tasted great. When I plopped my mug down on the bar and wiped my mouth with a napkin, my attention was drawn to some babbling coming from a drunk seated four stools to my left. I glanced toward the source of the babbling but didn't pay much attention to the man slumped over his drink. His wildly unkempt hair and beard along with his stained, ripped clothes gave him the appearance of a man who was either homeless or on the precipice of becoming homeless.

I turned back toward Hector, but now the drunk's words became understandable. "Hey Pete," he slurred, "do you smell something?"

Pete was at the corner of the bar flipping through the pages of a newspaper. "I don't smell anything," he replied without looking up from the paper.

"I smell something," the drunk continued, "and I think I know what it is."

"What is it?" the disinterested bartender asked.

"Garbage," the drunk declared. "Wait a minute." He turned and sniffed toward Hector and me. "It's garbage cops," he sneered.

Hector jumped off his stool. "Excuse me, buddy, do you have a problem?"

I threw my hand out to block Hector's path while Pete handled the situation. "Hey," Pete called out to the drunk, "that's enough for you today – time to go."

"I'm going – I'm going," the drunk slurred as he staggered out the door.

Hector and I returned to our beers and to congratulating ourselves on the triumphant first day of the warrant squad.

Pete approached our empty mugs. "Two more gentlemen?"

I looked at Hector and shrugged. "Why not?"

When the freshly filled mugs were in front of us, Hector had a question before he began working on his new beer. "You should look to get some new clientele in here, my friend."

Pete nodded. "You're right. That guy is nothing but trouble. I would have banned him for good after that stunt, but I didn't out of a courtesy to Jimmy."

I almost spit out the beer I was sipping. "What?" I gasped. "Why is giving some obnoxious drunk a break a courtesy to me?"

"Because I know he's your friend," Pete replied.

"Friend?" I was still clueless.

A wide smile grew on Pete's face. "You didn't recognize him, did you?"

"Recognize who?"

"That was Kevin," Pete said.

I jumped off the stool and ran to the door. I burst out onto the sidewalk and looked up and down Woodhaven Boulevard, but there was no sign of the unkempt drunk. I went back inside the Swagman and began rattling off question after question to Pete.

"Whoa – hold your horses Jimmy," Pete cautioned. "All I know is what I see, and you could see it to. The rags of his pants are beating him to death whenever he come in here."

"How often does he come in here?" I asked.

Pete shrugged. "On average I would say once a week. He usually throws a twenty on the bar and drinks until he's used up his money."

"Is he working?" I asked.

"Look, Jimmy," Pete explained. "I don't know anything else about where he works or lives, but you can see for yourself that he's not exactly doing well."

Pete walked away to serve another drunk at the other end of the bar.

"What the hell was that all about?" Hector asked.

I shook my head. "It's a long story – a very long story."

...

On day two of warrant squad operations Inspector Malloy's final words to us about future summonses having "teeth" became prophetic – in a strange and painful way.

Our first victim was the owner of a hair salon on Yellowstone Boulevard in Forest Hills. It was only 6:30 A.M., but this salon appeared active with the staff sitting on the terrace, passing the time with coffee. They never talked, not that I saw. I guess their way of living was one of constant chatter and so they relished this quiet time and willed it to stretch onwards. It was a simple place, one large room for the cutting and the outside terrace where the customers often waited, weather permitting.

At the counter was our scofflaw. She was an old woman but didn't look to be the kind you pity with their old bones and feeble limbs. This lady looked like she could still run an army kitchen given half a chance. She stood quite tall and slim, her short grey hair neat and likely styled with old fashioned rollers, the kind women used to sleep in. Her face was made up with discrete make-up except her lips that were cherry red. Were she any paler her mouth would be garish, but against her sun-kissed skin it looked right. When she extended her hand to shake mine, I saw the soil beneath her fingernails. I figured she spent a lot of time on the perimeter of the terrace tending to the flowers. Her smile was all sweetness as he greeted us. "How may I help you gentlemen?"

Hector extended his right hand to display the arrest warrant. "This is an arrest warrant, ma'am."

"That's nice," she nodded.

Hector continued. "I'm sorry to say that we are going to have to place you under arrest as a sanitation scofflaw."

"Oh, okay," she acknowledged in a voice just above a whisper. "Can I just take a closer look at your warrant?" she asked.

"Of course," Hector said as he moved his hand closer to her face.

It happened in an instant. The sweet, serene voice turned into a guttural growl, and the accompanying bite into Hector's hand would have made a junkyard dog proud.

"Ahhhhhhhh!" Hector screamed as the women's teeth dug into Hector's hand.

I jumped behind the woman and wrapped my arms around her waist, yanking her away from Hector with all my strength. She released her bite, and the force of my pull threw he to the floor in the corner of the salon floor.

As if someone had rung the bell to begin a wresting battle royale, the hair stylists who had been peacefully lounging on the terrace sipping coffee came flying into the salon to attack the already wounded Hector and me.

Under normal circumstances I would not have had a major problem with a couple of attractive young ladies crawling all over me, tearing at my clothes, but these girls were out for blood – my blood. My fight wasn't going well, but thankfully, a passerby on the sidewalk had seen Hector and me, struggling, with our shields dangling from chains around our necks, and called 911 to report plainclothes police officers in need of assistance.

The volume and number of sirens increased until finally the battling beauties were pulled off Hector and me by an army of responding cops. Hector was taken by ambulance to Elmhurst General Hospital to be treated for a human bite, while I was taken to the 112th Precinct to process the prisoners. The cops at the precinct were very helpful, but I had to endure more than one remark about how terrible it must have been to be smothered under those beautiful bodies.

Hector was back to work in a week and our warrant squad work continued with no further incidents. A full month into the operation we had made 57 scofflaw arrests, and we figured we had enough scofflaws on our list to keep working this warrant squad detail for the remainder of our careers. And then there was the call from Inspector Malloy.

"Hello, Jimmy Boy, how are you and Hector doing?"

"We're good, Inspector."

"How is Hector's hand?"

"Good as new," I replied.

"That's good to hear," Malloy said.

"And we really wanted to thank you," I continued. "This warrant squad assignment has been great."

"I hope not too great," Malloy sighed.

"Uh oh," I fretted, "that doesn't sound good."

"It's not that bad," the Inspector assured. "It's just that you've done such a great job. We've gotten coverage in the newspapers and on the TV news, so the commissioner feels the point has been made and that there is no real point in continuing to arrest scofflaws. People know now what can happen if they don't pay their fines."

"So, what are we being assigned to do?" I asked.

"You're gonna be my all-purpose team," Malloy said.

"What exactly does that mean, sir? I asked.

"I may still have you doing warrants now and then," Malloy explained, "when the point needs to be reinforced."

"What about when the point doesn't need to be reinforced?" I asked.

"Dumps," Malloy declared.

"Dumps?" I repeated.

We were seated in the steamy front seat of a van without air-conditioning. I peered through a pair of binoculars into the wilds of the Bronx frontier marked by trucking depots and factories, vacant lots, high grass, narrow streets and—to my chagrin—piles upon piles of illegally dumped refuse. I was here with Hector because Inspector Malloy told us that for years, the East River fringes of Hunts Point had been one of many targets of the Sanitation Police.

We were dressed more like truck drivers than police officers, armed with a list of some of the city's most infamous dumping spots in our territory, which covered all 43,000 acres of the Bronx and Manhattan. Our mission was simple, but often daunting and occasionally tinged with danger: Catch illegal dumpers in the act, apprehend them and write summonses that carry fines of up to $5,000. In most cases, we were also to impound the vehicles used in illegal dumping in case a violator would not or could not pay the fines.

According to Inspector Malloy, every year thousands of tons of garbage, from heaps of automobile tires to reeking mounds of rotting fruit rinds, were illegally left in New York streets and vacant lots. He explained that much of it was dumped by haulers who fattened their profit margins by charging to pick up refuse and then dumping it in vacant lots, by small contractors looking for an easy way to rid themselves of building waste and by residents not willing to wait for sanitation workers to pick up household bulk, like old furniture.

I eased the Ford down what appeared to be a dead-end street in Hunts Point, but it was actually a street blocked by a mound of discarded automobile parts, tires, sofa pillows and a chunk of a kitchen sink.

"Don't the sanitation trucks ever come through here?" I lamented.

"I worked up here, partner," Hector said. "They clean it quite a bit, but it's a losing battle."

"I would really like to catch all these guys," I fumed as I carefully maneuvered around another pile of freshly discarded stacks of wooden skids.

"I've got a general idea where they come from," said Hector said, "but I'm not really sure."

I backed the van between a nearby wall and a parked tractor-trailer. Hector and I sat like two fishermen, swapping tales about the dumpers and what we would do to make sure they didn't end up being the big one who got away. All the while, we watched and waited for anything suspicious to stir in the near distance.

Just before dusk, our storytelling ended abruptly when we noticed a battered 1972 Dodge van edging along the vacant lots near Manida Street and Viele Avenue. A young man leaped from the rear of the truck. Looking both ways, he apparently did not see our van sandwiched between the warehouse wall and truck about fifty yards away. In seconds, the man heaved large plastic bags packed with what later turned out to be orange peelings, into the lot. I quickly moved the van behind the Dodge van and its startled driver and passengers, while Hector loudly demanded that the van pull over.

We were out of the van, with badges drawn, and caught three Hispanic men who peddled fruit for a living. None of them spoke very much English and I didn't find out until that moment that Hector spoke very little Spanish. With the help of a bilingual officer at the 41st

Precinct station house, the matter was sorted out hours later. I wrote a summons for the owner of the van and seized his vehicle. The peddlers walked home with a new dread of the sanitation police and a box of unsold fruit.

"All in all," I said to Hector, "it wasn't such a bad day."

CHAPTER 9:

I enjoyed the various plainclothes assignments and Hector and I actually got our names in the paper when we made and arrest for a street robbery with a gun. Things were going well for a cop named Jimmy Murphy, and then it was Déjà vu all over again. This time, despite the fact that my old man's penmanship had not improved, I immediately recognized the name and number.

"Inspector Malloy, how can I help you?"

"Inspector," I sang, "It's Jim Murphy."

"Oh yes, Jimmy-Boy, how have you been?"

"I'm very good, sir," I said. "The job's been good, and I have you to thank for it."

"That's good to hear, Jim, because this is another one of those phone calls that going to rock your world."

All the muscles in my body tensed. "What do you mean, sir?"

"Well," Malloy sighed, "let me try to explain the situation as succinctly as possible. We don't have a detective division, but we do have investigators in our inspector general's office. Do you know about that unit?"

"I know it exists, but honestly, sir, I don't know much about it."

"Well," Malloy began, the inspector general investigates corruption, waste and mismanagement withing the department. It's like our version of internal affairs. We have members of the sanitation police detailed to the IG's office as investigators."

"I think I understand," I said.

"What you wouldn't know," Malloy began, "is that the Inspector General was arrested this morning and the entire IG staff has been dumped."

"Oh my God!" I gasped. "What did he do?"

"He stole bags."

"Bags?" my voice was an octave higher.

"That's right," Malloy explained, "Walter Brennan was accused of stealing 40,000 heavy duty trash bags worth $4,000. He's also accused of lying when he told the commissioner he sent him a report on the theft, when in actuality he had destroyed the report to cover up the fact that the investigation had yielded evidence suggesting that high officials in the sanitation department had taken the bags for their own use."

"Where did these bags come from?" I asked.

"The bags were part of 300,000 that were supposed to be distributed to the public during the threat of an impending sanitation strike. According to the commissioner, the bags were reported missing from a warehouse at Pier 99, at 59th Street and the Hudson River, where they were supposed to be given out through block associations and neighborhood groups. Last summer," Malloy continued, "a foreman at the warehouse reported that 40,000 bags were missing, and Inspector General Brennan ordered an investigation. A handwritten report of more than twenty pages was prepared by an investigator with the IG's office. The report indicated that department officials had taken 28,000 bags, while the rest were unaccounted for. The investigator's report contained photostats of inventory records that showed alterations in department records designed to conceal the shortage. The Department of Investigation, which had been alerted to the disappearance of the bags, subsequently received information that the Sanitation Department investigation was being improperly conducted," Malloy said.

"The Department of Investigation leaned on a sanitation man who worked at the Pier 99 warehouse and subsequently recorded a conversation between him and IG Brennan. During that conversation the Inspector General was heard to say that he personally threw the investigative report away."

"Is that all?" I asked.

"No," Malloy replied. "Brennan was also charged with staging a burglary at the warehouse in which tools and inventory records were stolen. As a result, Brennan was charged with reporting an incident that he knew had not occurred and with two counts of criminal solicitation, for allegedly asking the sanitation man to remove or destroy certain inventory books."

"I'm confused," I said. "What could the possible motive have been?"

"No one knows," Malloy replied, "but I doubt Brennan was going to try to resell them for profit."

"Maybe they were used for a good reason," I speculated, "like handing them out and making the community happy."

"How naïve young people can be?" Malloy snickered.

"How do I figure into this situation," I asked.

"Come to my office as soon as you can, Jim."

"I can be there in twenty minutes, sir, but why?"

"So, I can assign you to the Inspector General's squad."

"What?" I gasped.

"That's right," Malloy explained. "When the commissioner cleaned house, he eliminated our ability to perform any internal investigations. I have to get that office up and running with an investigative staff as soon as possible."

"Why me?" I asked.

"I'll explain everything when you get here. See you in twenty minutes, Jim."

Inspector Malloy's office was as small and cluttered as it was during my other visits. The stress was visible in all the new age lines and wrinkles on the Inspector's face as he remained seated and motioned for me to sit without offering a handshake.

"Thanks for getting here so quickly, Jim."

"No problem, sir," I said while settling into the uncomfortable chair in front of the Inspector's desk

Malloy folded his hands on the desktop. "I'll get right to it, Jim. You asked on the phone why you for the IG's squad."

"That's correct, sir."

"You've maintained a good record during your time with the department, both as a sanman and a cop with no complaints or charges against you."

"Thank you, sir," I replied, "but I don't even have two years yet as a police officer."

Malloy held up his index finger. "Let me finish," he cautioned. "More important than time on the job is the fact that you have a college degree."

My eyebrows raised. "Really?" I remarked. "Did all the police who were dumped have degrees?"

Malloy cleared his throat. "Actually, none of them had college."

I shook my head. "I don't understand, sir. If none of the previous investigators had college, why is my degree so important."

"The mayor recently signed an executive order mandating inspector generals in all city agencies. The sanitation department had an inspector general but not all the other agencies did." Malloy took a quick sip from a can of 7-Up that was on his desk. "The executive order directs the department of investigation to come up with the qualifications for the inspector generals and the investigators on their staffs." The Inspector shook his head and held up a piece of paper. "These qualifications do not require any investigative of law enforcement experience. The one basic requirement to be an IG investigator is a four-year college degree."

"Are there many other sanitation cops with degrees?" I asked.

Malloy shrugged. "Not many, but I'm still going through the personnel files. I haven't told you the main problem yet."

"And what might that be?" I asked.

"The IGs office is not being limited to members of the department. It is not required to be a member of the sanitation police to get assigned to the squad. As a matter of fact, the commissioner has already said that he wants the IG squad to be half sanitation police and half newly hired civilians with college degrees." Malloy leaned back and placed his hands behind his head. "So, you can see what's keeping me up at night, Jimmy Boy. I'm going to have to fill half the investigative staff in the IG's office with civilian college pukes while I struggle to come up with a few sanitation cops who have the college degree."

"I see your problem now," I nodded.

"So, when I find someone on the department who has the college, and who I know and think highly of, he's in whether he likes it or not." Malloy smiled. "But I do hope you like it."

"I'll do whatever you ask," I said.

"Good," Malloy nodded. "You'll report on Monday at 9 A.M. to 51 Chambers Street. It's right across the street from City Hall. The IG's office is on the 13th floor."

"The 13th floor?" I gulped.

"What's wrong," Malloy questioned, "are you superstitious?"

"Not in the least," I replied. "Who will I be reporting to?"

"That's a good question," the Inspector chuckled. "Hopefully, there will be an inspector general in place, but who knows?"

"Do I wear my uniform?"

"Of course not," Malloy scoffed, "You're a detective now. You wear soft clothes."

"What exactly are soft clothes?"

"Business attire – a shirt and tie," Malloy explained. He snapped the fingers on his right hand. "That's right. I almost forgot. You need a new shield. If you are going to be a detective, you'll need a detective's shield." He began fishing his hand through a drawer on the left side of his desk. He was mumbling in a low tone as he fished. "I could have sworn I still had some detective shields in here, but I guess not." His hand emerged from the drawer holding something gold. "Here," he said as he flipped the round gold object at me."

I made the catch and was immediately stunned. I was holding a gold sanitation police badge, but it wasn't the shield of a detective. "This is a lieutenant's shield," I stammered.

"Yeah," Malloy replied, "I guess I don't have any more detective shields."

I took a couple of deep breaths and tried to choose my next words carefully. Very slowly and deliberately I asked THE question. "So, does this mean I'm a lieutenant?"

Inspector Malloy curled his lip and appeared to be in deep thought for a moment. Suddenly, he slapped both hands down on his desk and announced, 'Why not – you're a lieutenant."

I swayed side to side in the chair as I tried to absorb what was going on. "Is this legal?" I asked in a loud whisper.

"Legal?" Malloy laughed. "Why wouldn't it be legal?" You keep forgetting your civil service status. You're a sanitation man and you're paid as a sanitation man. I could make you a sergeant, lieutenant, captain, or brigadier general for that matter, and you'll still be a sanitation man."

"Well, I thank you anyway, sir," I said.

The Inspector smiled. "You just asked me who you would be reporting to. There's a good chance now that people may be reporting to you. Keep those college pukes in line."

"But I don't have any investigative experience," I shrugged.

"But they don't know that," Malloy grinned. "Good luck, Lieutenant."

...

Sunday evening at eight o'clock I sat on my living room sofa watching TV, but my mind was miles away. Specifically, I was focused on the next morning and my new home at 51 Chambers Street.

"Stop doing that," Kristen warned, "I can't concentrate on the show."

"What am I doing?" I asked.

"Your leg is jumping up and down like the piston in a car," she giggled.

"Sorry," I said, "I guess I'm just nervous about tomorrow."

Kristin put her head on my shoulder. "That's okay sweetie. You'll be fine tomorrow. Try to relax and watch the show. It's gonna be good tonight."

Kristin's soothing words along with her head resting on my shoulder relaxed me instantly, but the last thing I wanted to do was concentrate on the TV show. Kristin and I had a lot in common, but as far as a favorite TV show was concerned, we were polar opposites. Hardcastle and McCormack was a ridiculous crime drama about a vigilante-type old judge who every week brought his own brand of justice to those criminals who had gotten off the hook on legal technicalities. The plots were terrible, and the acting was horrible, but Kristen liked the show, so I put up with it.

Just as the judge, played by Brian Keith, was about to hand out another heaping helping of justice to a horrible thug, I received a pardon from the governor in the form of a ringing phone.

"Excuse me, babe," I whispered, giving Kristin a chance to lift her head off my shoulder.

"Hello."

"Hello, Jim, It's Inspector Malloy. Sorry to bother you on a Sunday night."

"This can't be good," I chuckled.

"Come on, Jim," Malloy shot back, "You're making me sound like the grim reaper."

"I'm sorry, sir."

"No need to apologize, Jim. I just wanted to give you a heads up about tomorrow."

"Good news, I hope."

"That depends on your perspective," Malloy said.

"Oh, boy," I sighed.

"Here's the deal, Jim," Malloy began. There will be an inspector general in place in the office tomorrow."

"Well, that is good news," I responded.

"His name is Andrew Broderick."

"What do you know about him?" I asked.

"Not much," Malloy replied. "I know he's lawyer because that was the qualification to be an inspector general,"

"Okay," I said. "How many other cops did you find with college degrees?"

"Two," Malloy replied.

"So, there will be a total of three members of the sanitation police in the squad." I speculated.

"Hang on, Jimmy Boy," Malloy cautioned. "I said I found two with degrees. I never said they were being assigned to the IG's office."

"I don't understand."

"When I made them the same offer you received – you know, the offer they couldn't refuse. Do you know what happened?"

"What?"

"They refused."

"But you said..."

"I know what I said," Malloy interrupted, "but these guys said they'd go back to tossing cans behind a truck before they would work for the rat squad."

"Rat squad?" I squealed.

"Come on, Jimmy," Malloy laughed. "Are you trying to tell me you never heard that affectionate nickname before."

"No, I haven't."

"Well, it comes with the territory, young man. Remember, we're just like internal affairs in the NYPD, and they are called the rat squad too, and a lot worse."

There was a momentary silence on the line until the Inspector spoke again. "Please don't tell me you're gonna back out on me now."

"No," I sighed. "I said I'd do it, so I'm still in."

"That's great," Malloy said, "and I think I have something you'll consider to be good news."

"I can't wait." I groaned.

"When I told the commissioner I could only find one candidate from the ranks of the sanitation police, he asked me what rank was that candidate. When I told him you were a lieutenant, he was thrilled."

"Why was he thrilled?" I asked.

"Because he had a new plan for the office that these circumstances fit perfectly."

"What plan?"

"The commissioner wants only one member of the sanitation police to be part of the IG's squad, and he wants that member to be a sergeant or lieutenant who will perform the function of chief investigator. The investigative staff will all be civilian college pukes."

"Are you telling me that I am the chief investigator?"

"That's right."

"But I've never even been an investigator – anywhere."

"Ssshhh, don't say that so loud," Malloy cautioned. "You and I are the only people who know that."

"Well, it's gonna be pretty clear to everyone else real soon," I announced.

"Investigations are not brain surgery," Malloy said. "Just read all the old case files and use them as a template. And remember, as little as you think you know, those college pukes know less. Good luck, chief investigator."

I hung up the phone and stared at nothing in particular on the other side of the living room."

"Are you okay?" Krisin asked.

"Just wonderful," I sighed.

CHAPTER 10:

Even though I was told to report to my new assignment at 9 A.M., I was walking up Chambers Street at 7:45. I wanted to make sure there was no way I would be late. I stopped on the sidewalk and scratched my head. I counted 17-stories to this very vintage-looking building that resembled the letter "H." One of the wings had the address 49 while the other read 51. Above the 51 was a façade with the words Emigrant Industrial Savings Bank engraved in stone.

The lobby was large and ornate like I had seen in some old movies and the elevator actually had an operator who opened and closed cage-like doors on each floor.

When I left the elevator on the 13th floor it suddenly occurred to me that my wonderful investigative instincts had failed to ask Inspector Malloy for the office number or where I was supposed to find a key to ender the office. The first problem was solved when I turned left in the hallway and on the first door on the left was conspicuous lettering on the frosted glass door that read "Department of Sanitation Inspector General."

I knocked on the door but could hear no signs of life or activity coming from the inside of the office. I was thinking about how I would find the building superintendent when those keen investigative instincts I hoped to find commanded me to try the doorknob. Sure enough, the knob turned, and the door opened.

I stuck my head inside and looked both ways. The air was motionless in the office and the smell of old papers and dust hung in the air. Directly ahead of me was a desk that was probably used by a receptionist. To the left was a small hall the appeared to contain doors to two small offices. To the right the hall entered into a large inner office with desks lining the walls. This was obviously the investigator's room. I made a complete sweep of the entire office to make sure I was alone.

Moving around that empty old office immediately transported me back in time. The faded, peeling wallpaper, and the creaky wooden floorboards gave it an aged feel. Even when I flipped the switches I could find, the office was dimly lit, with a few overhead fluorescent bulbs casting a pale, eerie light throughout the space.

The desks in the two private offices and around the perimeter of the larger investigator's room were made of dark, heavy wood, and the drawers were rusted and difficult to open. The chairs were made of leather and had seen better days, with rips and tears that gave them a worn-out appearance.

I stood in the center of the large investigator's room and made a slow 360-degree turn, taking in a very surreal scene. On two desks there were partially filled ice-cold cups of coffee and on two other desks were open file folders containing handwritten notes and typed pages. On another desk there was a typewriter containing a piece of paper where the typing seemed to have stopped in the middle of a sentence. Suddenly, the scene made sense to be. The investigators were working at their desks when they were told they were dumped from the IG's office. They weren't even given time to finish a cup of coffee of put case folder back in the filing cabinets.

Two old metal file cabinets were wedged between a couple of the desks. Stains and dents marred the once shiny gray finish of the cabinets, pitted with age. I pulled on the drawer handles, but they wouldn't open. It would be just my luck that the vital case folders would be the only things in the office that were locked. I decided to take the scientific approach to opening the cabinet. I slammed my shoulder into the drawer handles and winced when I made contact, but the drawers didn't budge. Undaunted, I gathered myself and slammed into the cabinet once more, harder than before. There was a dull crack as if something had broken. I was less interested in what I may have damaged and more interested in the fact that the drawers were now freely opening.

Those keen investigative instincts I was hoping existed inside me were screaming that these file cabinets were the key. They were stuffed full of case folders that would be able to tell me exactly what the investigators in this office did and how they did it. I removed a hand full of folders from the top drawer and plopped them down on the adjacent desktop. I sat at the desk, opened the top folder, and began reading. I had flipped through three pages in the investigative folder when my Spidey Sense began to tingle. I looked quickly to the left and discovered I wasn't alone. There was a man standing in the threshold between the hall and the large investigator's room.

"Well, hello," The man greeted.

He had dark hair and a mustache that connected to his goatee. He was wearing a blue long sleeve shirt and blue jeans. I guess his definition of soft clothes was different than the one I had received. He wasn't wearing a belt and his pants were sagging low enough to reveal a small amount of untanned stomach.

He was short and thin and appeared to be in his thirties. There was something a little hippy-ish about him, from the way he moved to his slightly long hair. He looked for all the world like he was walking to his own beat, literally, like there was music playing in his head.

I closed the file folder. "Good morning."

"And who might you be?" the man asked.

"Lieutenant Jim Murphy, Sanitation Police"

The man extended his hand. "Andy Broderick. I'm the new Inspector General."

"It's a pleasure to meet you, sir?" I said.

Broderick squinted and wagged his index finger in my direction. "Wait a minute. Are you my chief investigator?"

"Yes sir."

Broderick eyed me from head to toe. "You're kind of young to be a lieutenant and a chief investigator, aren't you?"

I don't know where it came from, but I blurted out a response immediately. "You're kind of young to be a lawyer and an inspector general, aren't you?"

Broderick stroked his chin and smiled. "Touché," he said. "But I assure you," he continued, I have been a member of the New York Bar for three years."

"So," I let the word draw out unnaturally long. "How will this office operate."

"You're asking me?" Broderick laughed. "You're the chief investigator – you tell me."

I took a step back and cocked my head as if to make sure he said what I thought he said. "You haven't handled anything like this before? How could that be? You are here to investigate corruption in government – surely that is not something new to you. What kind of cases have you tried?" I asked.

"Personal injury – mostly slips and falls. Very few go to trial. Most of them settle." Broderick's grin grew wider. "Now, I'll ask you again, Chief Investigator, how do we get this office up and running?

"Well," I shrugged, "I suppose we should get everyone settled in the office. There are two offices on the other side that I assume are for me and you. When the investigators arrive, we can get them settled in desks and go from there. I was going to read these case folders to get the flavor of the cases they worked here."

"Sounds good," Broderick replied. "So, you don't think I am totally useless, I do have some information."

I stifled a chuckle, attempting to be diplomatic as I responded. "I never said you were useless,"

Broderick cleared his throat before continuing. "When I was hired, I had to meet with the chief of staff at the department of investigation. He described the process, how DOI works as a clearing house for all cases involving the city's inspector generals. Their intake unit receives and assigns cases every 24-hours. When our investigators finish an assigned case, we forward the final report back to DOI."

I nodded, impressed at how efficient and organized it all sounded. "That seems doable."

"Let's hope so," Broderick replied.

He pointed down the hallway to the private offices. "I guess we should get settled in our offices before the investigators arrive."

"Yes, sir," I agreed.

Broderick held up his hand. "Please, the last time anyone called me sir was when I played Lancelot in my high school production of King Arthur. So, you don't have to call me sir, sire, or your majesty. My name is Andy."

"Okay, sir...I mean Andy."

Andy led the way down the hall and peeked inside the two offices. He turned and smiled at me. "I'll take the large office and you can have the closet."

I frowned but didn't say anything as I walked to the smaller office at the end of the hall. The door was unlocked, and when I opened it, I was instantly transported to Inspector Malloy's tiny office in Queens. The former occupant must have had some advance warning of his demise because unlike the investigator's office that seemed to be frozen in time, this office had been stripped clean. The only decoration in the bare room was a place where a picture frame used to hang, leaving behind a darker area on a wall speckled with chipping paint. The worn wood desk was empty both in the drawers and on the desktop, and the metal file cabinet was also empty.

"I'd step inside your office, but I might create a dangerous crowd condition," Andy chuckled from my office doorway.

I noted the 9:10 A.M. time on my watch. "I wish we did have a crowd right now. What the heck happened to the investigators who are supposed to be here?

Andy snapped his fingers. "That's right," he blurted. "I knew there was something I forgot to tell you."

"What?"

"DOI told me that they told the four investigators we are getting to report on Wednesday morning."

"Well, I guess that's good news," I shrugged. "It will give me two days to read all those case folders so I can try to convince these investigators I know what I'm talking about."

...

Over the next two days I sat inside my tiny office surrounded by towering stacks of file folders, hoping I could become a sponge. Each folder contained notes and reports prepared by the recently departed investigative team. I read case folder after case folder trying to absorb every detail I could about the investigations. By the afternoon of the second day, I had my notes separated into two columns. The first column indicated the types of investigations performed and the second reflected the format used to record the work.

There were many different subjects covered in the folders I perused, but thankfully, many of them had similar themes. The subject that repeated itself most often was "trade waste." The sanitation department did not pick up trash from businesses. Merchants were required to contract with a private carting service for their trash removal, and to post a sticker identifying their carter in the business window. For smaller businesses and stores, the expense of a private carter could put a strain on the business, so the owners would sometimes try to pay the local sanitation crew to take their "trade waste."

There were also investigations performed regarding sick leave. Sanitation men, like the uniformed members of the police and fire departments enjoyed the benefit of unlimited sick leave. Along with this fantastic benefit came the potential for abuse by scammers who could fake illnesses indefinitely. Therefore, strict controls were placed on members of the sanitation department who called out sick, the most basic of which was the requirement for sanitation men out sick to stay inside their residence. There was a unit of foreman whose job it was to visit the residences of members out sick to ensure they were home. These foremen handled the investigations of sanmen who were caught out of their homes while out sick. The inspector general's investigators became involved when another element was present. I found several folders that reflected investigations of sanman out sick who were alleged to be working other jobs or running businesses while they were out sick.

I also found a very seasonal type of investigation. Besides collecting trash, the sanitation department was responsible for snow removal on city streets – emphasis on "city streets." During the winter months when it snowed there were cases in the file folders involving sanmen plowing streets who allegedly detoured off their plowing route to accept some easy cash to plow private driveways and parking lots.

When Andy and I left the office at the end of the day I hoped I had absorbed enough from the case folders to at least make it look like I knew what I was talking about. I would get my answer to that question the next morning.

At 9:00 A.M. I stood in the center of the investigator's room next to Andy. We turned slowly 360 degrees as if we were one unit, nodding and smiling at the four freshly minted investigators sitting at the desks that were pushed up against each wall in the room.

I readied myself for a long welcoming speech from Andy, but he left me with my mouth hanging wide open when he said, "Welcome aboard everyone. Chief Investigator Murphy will fill you in on the details of your new jobs."

Andy smiled, slapped my back and retreated to the safety of his office, leaving me standing alone in the center of the large room. I shuffled my feet back and forth and cleared my throat. "Well, it's good to see everyone this morning. How is everyone doing?" I made a 360-degree turn and was met by silence and blank stares.

"Why don't we get to know each other a little bit," I suggested. I pointed to the male sitting directly in front of me. He had a baby face that made him look like he could still be in high school. He was dressed conservatively in a white shirt, navy blue tie, black trousers, and black dress shoes. He had short, dark hair parted on the side and he was slim and appeared tall, although I could not be sure of his height while he was sitting. "Why don't you start us off. Tell me your name and a little bit about yourself."

The male looked down to the floor as he mumbled in a tone consistent with a loud whisper. "My name is Will Perry from Astoria."

There was a moment of silence until I realized I would have to prompt more information. "What about your school and work experience, Will?"

Will's focus remained on the floor. "I just graduated from John Jay with a bachelor's in Criminal Justice. The only prior job I ever had was a paper route when I was 14-years-old."

I nodded and smiled. "Thanks, Will." I pointed to the right. "You're next." I did a double take when I noticed the size of this person. There was an audible creaking sound coming from the chair that looked like it was ready to collapse at any second. It seemed miraculous that he was able to fit his girth into the chair in the first place. This gentleman quickly dispelled the stereotype that all fat people are jolly with the tone of his greeting.

"My name is Greg Wilson," he snarled. "I qualified for this job with a bachelor's degree and anything else about me is my personal business."

"Suit yourself," I shrugged. "Welcome aboard."

I made an about face to focus my attention on the two people seated on the other side of the room. I nodded at the well-dressed young female with the horned rimmed glasses and dark hair tied back in a tight bun.

"Good morning," she began, "my name is Liz Hanson."

I would describe her appearance at best as homely, but as she spoke, she exuded a sense of confidence and poise. From the tailored cut of her clothing to her precise application of makeup and jewelry, she displayed an aesthetic that emphasized her attention to detail.

I returned to focusing on her words as she was finishing up. "So, although I don't have any prior work experience, I'm looking forward to putting all my energy into being successful in this new adventure."

"Adventure," Greg muttered under his breath from the other side of the room. "What are we, pirates?"

I twisted my torso and held up my right index finger. "You had your turn, Greg. Give everyone else a chance."

"Thanks Liz, it's great to have you on board." I pointed to the last new investigator. My eyes widened as I took my first good look at this young man. He appeared to be tall, even while seated. His skin was as pale as a glass of milk, making it look even whiter when contrasted by his jet-black slicked back hair. There was something sinister about his dark sunken eyes, as if he was lurking in the shadows like a cobra seeking its prey. When he opened his mouth, I was prepared for a Bela Lugosi style "Good evening," but I couldn't have been more off base.

"Good morning, everyone," he chirped. "I'm Walter Sloan, a recent criminal justice graduate from John Jay, and I live in Brooklyn. I do have some prior work experience."

"Excellent," I said. "Tell us about it."

"I started at Flatbush Lanes Bowling Alley working at the snack bar and was promoted to customer service representative."

"That means you got to spray disinfectant into the bowling shoes." Greg mocked.

"Actually, that was one of my duties," Walter smiled, "but I was responsible for a lot more."

"Like polishing the bowling pins," Greg snickered.

"Okay," I said, "I think that's enough. I'm sure we'll get to know each other much better as time goes on."

I proceeded to spend the remainder of the morning telling my new staff all about the types of investigations they would be handling and how they would be recording them.

"There are two unmarked cars assigned to the IG's office, "I explained. "One car is parked in the Queens West 1 garage on 21st Street in Astoria and the other is Bronx 11 on Zerega Avenue." I glanced momentarily at all my staff members. "I'm gonna divide you into two teams – a Brooklyn/Queens team and a Manhattan/Bronx team. I'll decide who will handle Staten Island cases as they come up." I pointed to Will and Walter. "You guys will be the Brooklyn/Queens team. You'll pick up the car at the district in Astoria and either come into the office or go on your cases in the field."

Walter and Will looked at each other and nodded.

"Liz and Greg will be the Manhattan/Bronx team and pick up their car in the Bronx each day."

"Wait a minute," Greg moaned. "That's great for her – she lives in the Bronx. I live in the ass end of Brooklyn."

I shrugged and tried unsuccessfully not to smile. "Then I guess you should have revealed some of your personal business."

I had given the new investigators all I could. I just hoped it was enough to make them believe their chief investigator knew what he was talking about. I took a long sip from the can of coke that always seemed to be on my desk. I closed my eyes to enjoy a few seconds of complete silence.

"Sleeping on the job already?"

My eyes flew open to the sight of Andy smiling in my doorway. "I was just enjoying a moment of quiet," I explained.

"Uncle Andy has something you can enjoy – work for our crack investigators."

"Finally," I sighed. "What is it?"

"The commissioner's office wants a couple of surveys completed forthwith."

"Surveys – what kind of surveys?" I questioned.

"I just got off the phone with the commissioner's office," Andy said as he dropped a legal pad on my desk. "I wrote all the details on the pad. Study the details for a few minutes, finish your coke and then go deploy the troops."

I stood in the center of the investigator's room holding the legal pad.

"Liz and Greg, I have a Manhattan job for you that comes straight from the commissioner's office," I said.

Liz sat up straight at her desk. "Great, what's the job?"

"It's a survey," I replied.

"What kind of a survey?" Liz asked.

"Litter baskets," I declared.

Liz recoiled in her chair. "Litter baskets?"

"This should be good," Greg mumbled from the other side of the room."

I inhaled in preparation of addressing the snide remark but changed my mind and returned my focus to Liz.

"The commissioner's office has received numerous complaints about the unavailability of litter baskets in Manhattan and he feels people may be stealing them."

"Garbage thieves," Greg guffawed. "I guess I should have realized what I was getting into."

"Hey!" I called across the room, "why don't you just pipe down and listen."

"Sure thing, boss," Greg said as he performed a mock salute from his chair.

"So, what exactly does this survey require us to do?" Liz asked.

"You're going to go from 14th street to 96th street from river to river and see if there are littler baskets on all four corners of every intersection."

"Do you know how long that's gonna take in Manhattan traffic," Greg roared.

"I forced a smile. "You're absolutely right, Greg. That's why you'll conduct this survey on the midnight shift."

"Wonderful," Greg moaned as he turned his back to me.

"A question, Chief," Liz interjected.

"Yes, Liz"

"What will we include in our survey report?"

"Your report will include a count of all the litter baskets as well as the locations where baskets are missing. For example, you might list southeast corner 59th street and Lexington Avenue."

"Got it," Liz nodded.

"I didn't know you had to be a math major to do this job." Greg said. "I hope my partner has math skills because I don't know if I'm gonna be able to count that high."

"Make believe you're counting donuts," Walter quipped.

"Very funny, Count Dracula," Greg shot back.

I held my hands high in the air. "Okay that's it," I bellowed. "You're all gonna get along if it kills you!"

Liz looked at me and smiled. "Don't worry, Chief. I have it covered."

I took a couple of deep breaths to compose myself. "Okay," I said, "I have another survey for you two boys."

"What do they have to do?" Greg scoffed, "count rats?"

Once again, I let the remark pass and continued giving Will and Walter their assignment. "With the water shortage the city has been experiencing, the commissioner wants to make sure the sanitation department is doing its part in avoiding being wasteful."

"What do you want us to do?" Walter asked.

"Visit facilities in Brooklyn and Queens and inspect them for unnecessary running water and leaks."

"What facilities should we inspect?"

"I'm not sure," I shrugged. "The survey request didn't specify. Just pick two facilities in Brooklyn and two in Queens."

"You got it Chief," Walter said.

When I got back into my office, it suddenly occurred to me that I liked being called chief.

...

I sat at my desk, surrounded by piles of papers that had somehow managed to spring up like fast growing plants. On this morning, however, I was not concerned with the mess on my desktop. My eyes were glued to one document sitting on top of a pile. Walter and Will had completed their water survey and I was about to review my first investigative report as Chief Investigator. I snatched the report from the pile, and immediately noticed that it was written in the proper format the investigators were told to use. So far, so good. My spirits soared as I began reading. The report was well written, with clear and concise language that was easy to understand. The report also had a logical structure, with the information presented in a way that made sense.

The report about unnecessary running water and leaks was full of interesting insights and data that I hadn't considered. Walter and Will had done an excellent job of analyzing the data and presenting it in a way that was both informative and engaging. As I read on, I found myself nodding along in agreement with their conclusions. The report was so well written that I felt like I was having a conversation with Walter and Will rather than just reading a dry, technical survey.

I was proud of Walter and Will, and of myself for laying out the assignment in such a way that they could produce such a fantastic result. My elation balloon popped in my face when I took note of the locations that had been the subject of the survey. My hands were trembling along with my voice. "Walter – Will," I bellowed. "Get in here, now!"

I immediately heard fast footsteps followed by the appearance of the two investigators at my office door.

"Morning, Chief," Walter greeted. "What's up?"

I waved the report in my right hand. "I just finished reading your survey."

Will smiled. "What did you think?"

I grit my teeth. "I think you two are morons."

The smiles disappeared from their faces. "What's wrong?" Walter asked. "We thought we did a pretty good job with the survey."

"Oh, you did a fantastic job," I nodded. "And I'm sure the Wonder Bread factory and Dante's Catering Hall are thrilled to know that they don't have any unnecessary running water."

"I don't understand, "Will said.

"This is the Department of Sanitation," I groaned. "This survey is for sanitation department facilities, not bread factories and wedding reception halls."

"To be fair," Will began, "you never specifically said..."

Walter must have seen the color of my face changing and cut his partner off before it became an even deeper shade of red. "Forget it," he said. "We'll go out right now and do the survey with two other facilities." He pushed Will out the door but before he cleared my doorway Walter turned and smiled. "And they will be sanitation facilities."

I scanned my desktop and grabbed my security blanket, which in this case was my can of Coke. The enjoyment of that long, cool sip was interrupted by the sounds of some type of commotion coming from the investigator's room. I could make out Walter's voice above the rest. "Excuse me?" he shouted. "Why don't you get up from that chair and say it to my face – if you're able to get out of the chair, you fat slob!"

"What the hell is going on in there?" Andy called out from his office.

"I don't know," I called back as I sprung from behind my desk, "but I', gonna find out right now."

The confrontation seemed to be escalating as I entered the room. Liz and Will were trying to get between the combatants to calm them down, but Walter and Greg were so focused on their own grievances that they didn't notice anyone else in the room.

Finally, Greg shoved Walter as he attempted to rise from his chair, causing Walter to stumble back, knocking over a stack of papers on Liz's desk. Walter lunged at Greg, and they started to physically fight. Will and Liz were stunned, and I didn't know what to do either.

My moment of indecision passed quickly as I jumped into the fray to break up the fight. I pulled them apart and ordered them both to neutral corners of the office.

"I'm tired of his big mouth," Walter griped.

Greg threw his arms out to the side. "All I said was that if he was checking for leaks everywhere in the city, he could come to my house and check my plumbing. The man's got no sense of humor."

"Both of you, shut up!" I roared. "I want both of you to get out of here. Either kill each other or come back when you've figured out how to work here in a civilized manner."

Walter and Greg departed while Will helped Liz retrieve the papers that had been knocked off her desk.

Andy appeared behind me and whispered in my ear. "Do you think that was a smart idea to send them out to the street together."

"I guess we'll find out soon enough," I sighed.

Twenty minutes later I breathed a huge sigh of relief when Greg and Walter returned to the office, both expressing embarrassment about their behavior. Even though the situation had de-escalated, I could still feel the tension in the office. Something else had to be done.

"Everybody listen up," I announced. "I have an assignment for everyone this afternoon that's gonna involve overtime." I paused for a moment and looked over to Andy, who was standing in the doorway to the investigators room. "As long as overtime is okay"

"Sure," he shrugged. "Why not?"

I turned to address the seated investigator's. "We're all going out to dinner together. Anybody have suggestions where we can go that's not too expensive,"

Walter raised his hand. "I know a few places in the East Village" he suggested,

The East Village was only a couple of miles from Chambers Street, but it may have well been on a different planet. The neighborhood was an international mecca for artists, musicians, writers as well as drifters, punks, homeless kids, and anyone who genuinely wanted to live in an environment where anything goes, and nobody was going to tell you no.

"There's a new place on St. Mark's Place that just opened," Walter said.

"What's the name?" I asked.

"I'm not sure," Walter replied, "but it has a zombie motif."

"Zombie?" I gasped.

"Sure," Walter nodded. "Zombies are a big thing in pop culture. Haven't you seen any zombie movies?"

"Like what?" I asked.

"The first one I saw was an old movie from 1932 called White Zombie," Walter said. "It starred Bela Lugosi."

Greg snapped his fingers. "I knew there was a connection between Lugosi and this guy." Greg held up his hands. "Just kidding."

"Very funny," Walter snickered. "Just like I knew there was a connection between you and the Goodyear Blimp – just kidding."

"Okay, okay, get back to the movies," I directed.

"You must have heard of Night of the Living Dead and Dawn of the Dead." Walter said.

"I heard of them," I shrugged, "But I never saw them."

"I saw one of them," Liz frowned. "The movie was disgusting."
"Oh, come on," Walter shot back, "it's a classic."

"Let's forget the movie reviews," I interrupted. "Is the food good and cheap?"

"Yes, on both accounts," Walter nodded.
"Good," I said, "Let's go."

CHAPTER 11:

The New York City Sanitation Police official parking permit was essential, but even then, it took ten minutes to find an illegal parking space adjacent to a fire hydrant. St. Mark's Place was teeming with activity. The team followed Walter while I took in the atmosphere of the street. The sidewalk seemed to be filled with 19th century farmers, all sporting beards, plaid flannel shirts, and vintage work boots. A beehive of instrument-bearing musicians and nose-pierced locals loitered in front of storefronts while an armada of young punks and artists competed with motor vehicles for dominance of the road.

Walter stopped and pointed to the ground floor of a newly constructed multi-use building that was surrounded by crumbling, decrepit early 20th century structures. Below the pricey new apartments was a large menu affixed to a glass window. The sign reminded those who stopped for inspection to "Eat Burgers, Not Brains."

"That's not funny," Liz scowled.

"Of course, it is," Walter corrected. "And the food is supposed to be fantastic."

Hundreds of conversations in loud voices competed for dominance of the atmosphere with loud rock music. While waiting to be seated I marveled at the motif. Without doubt it was the ugliest I had ever seen complete with barbed wire and heavily graffitied concrete cinder blocks. I shook my head. This was a brand- new building so this horrendous décor must have been by design.

The hostess was detestable to look at. Contact lenses gave the appearance of dirty yellow eyes that looked void and empty of life. Her skin had been made up to look like crinkled paper and her lips were the color of rusted iron. When she smiled, rotting yellow teeth were on full display and veins were splattered like red paint all over her face and hands.

A sweet British accent emerged from this horrible creature. "Follow me and I'll get you seated." Everyone but Walter seemed stunned as the hostess placed five menus on the table and completed her greeting. "The server will be with you in a minute. Enjoy your dinner."

Walter scanned the group. "Is this great?" he asked.

Liz pushed the menu away from her. "This is terrible!"

Walter waved dismissively at Liz and looked at me. "What do you think, Chief?"

I shrugged. "It's unique, I guess."

"It's ridiculous," Greg blurted.

"Amen to that," Will concurred.

The lively chatter at the table was interrupted by the arrival of the waitress, a female zombie with ponytailed blonde hair, decaying body, blue skin and wearing a tattered pink blouse, and green skirt under an orange apron. She smiled widely through her undead face. "Are you ready to order?"

Walter grabbed a menu. "Let's see," he said as he scanned the selections. "The brain burger looks good."

The waitress scribbled on her pad. "Would you like intestine fries with the burger?"

"Of course," Walter replied.

Liz's face was taking on the shade of the waitress. "I think I'm gonna be sick."

Thirty minutes later the team put the finishing touches on the banquet. Even Liz had to admit the food had been excellent. "This chicken was absolutely delicious."

"What did I tell you," Walter nodded.

"The food is great," Liz explained, "but the décor is still tasteless."

"She's right," Greg commented. "I don't care how good the food is. This place sucks, and that's coming from a fat bastard like me."

Walter took a deep breath in preparation of a response, but I beat him to the punch. "All right, all right, enough with this crap. Let's talk about something else."

Walter shrugged. "Fine with me. Ok, Chief, why don't you tell us about yourself."

"What?"

Liz smiled. "Come on. Tell us the dark secrets of your life."

"Let's see," I leaned back and scratched my head. "I joined the Sanitation Department three years ago, and..."

"Not about the job," Liz corrected. "About you."

I took a deep breath and glared at Liz. "Ok. I wanted to be a cop from the day a cop told off a miserable old man on my block who would steal my gang's rubber balls every time they bounced into his yard. But I couldn't pass the NYPD vision test, so I became a sanitation man and eventually got onto the sanitation police as a consolation prize." I looked at Liz. "How's that?"

Liz's demeanor had suddenly become sheepish. "Sorry about your NYPD dream," she commented as she sipped her beer. "We have something in common," she said as she tapped her horned rim glasses. "I wanted to be a cop too, but..."

"Your vision, too," I acknowledged.

"That's rich," Greg chuckled. "You two wanted to be cops and you ended up investigating garbage. I love it."

"Okay, funny guy," I snarled. "Let's hear your story.

"Let's see," Greg stroked his chin. "I like to work out and run marathons." He shook his head. "No, I guess you wouldn't believe that. I slept my way through four years of college and wanted to get some job just to prove the four years wasn't a total waste of time." He raised his eyebrows and smiled. "I never thought I'd end up with sanitation's rat squad."

"Where did you hear that?" I blurted.

"Hear what?" Greg replied.

"Rat squad."

"Everyone's heard that," Greg shrugged. "That's what we do, isn't it - rat out members of the department?"

I shook my head vigorously. "No, we investigate corruption and misconduct."

"Well," Greg smiled, "you call it what you want and the rest of the world will call us the rat squad. Get over it, Chiefy," Greg continued, "the two boys still have to make their speeches."

I drained my mug of Coors and looked at Walter. "What about you?"

"Nothing special about me," he shrugged. "I'm just looking to make my way in the world."

"Do you have any hobbies or interests?" I asked.

"I like haunted houses," Walter said. "I try to plan vacations around where I can visit a haunted house."

Greg pointed his finger at Walter. "You see, I was right. This goon fits my perception of a ghoul perfectly."

"You should stop talking," Walter suggested. "There's still more food on the table for you to inhale."

"Be nice, Walter," I reinstructed.

"That's okay, Chiefy," Greg said as he grabbed a roll from the basket. "He's right," he said just before plunging the entire roll into his mouth. "I'm beginning to like that guy," Greg garbled as he chewed the bread.

"You're closing the show." I said to Will.

Will maintained a stiff military bearing in his chair. "My grandfather and my father were doctors."

"You must be the black sheep of the family," Greg joked.

Will didn't laugh, but he didn't seem annoyed either. "When I was getting ready for medical school, my father had a bad heart attack. He lingered for three days, and the last thing he did was to beg me to take care of my mother. So, he died, and I looked for a job instead of med. school."

Liz reached across the table and patted the back of Will's hand. "I'm very sorry for your loss."

"Yeah, that sucks," Greg added.

Will snickered. "I do know something that would make me happy right now – another beer. Where's that zombie waitress for another round?"

Everyone laughed as the light small talk at the table continued. As the evening wore on, I noticed a strange phenomenon. Everyone seemed to be enjoying themselves.

CHAPTER 12:

Walter and Will got it right and found some sanitation facilities to check for leaks and running water and Liz and Greg turned in a great looking survey of the litter basket situation in Manhattan, complete with nicely drawn diagrams, which I'm sure were done by Liz. My ship seemed to be back in calm waters and was sailing full steam ahead.

Weeks turned into months as the cases passed through my desk. My crew was doing a very good job with the reports, although I was finding that the cases were very one dimensional. Many of the reports were for allegations of discourtesy by a sanman to a member of the public, and a significant amount were trade waste cases where it was alleged that sanitation crews were picking up commercial trash. Then one day Andy came into my office with a smile on his face and his legal pad in his hand.

He threw the pad on my desk and shook his hand. "Ow! He shrieked.

"What's wrong?" I asked.

"That was hot," he replied.

"Really?" I said.

"It's an allegation that a sanman who has been out sick for several months is routinely out of his residence without authorization."

"What's so hot about that?" I asked. "Why don't the foremen in the Sick Investigation Unit handle it.?."

"Because," Andy explained, "there's more to it."

"Like what?"

"Like the sanman is allegedly running his own body shop while he's out sick."

"That is interesting," I nodded. "I'm gonna give this to Walter and Will, but I think I'm gonna go out on this with them."

"Be my guest," Andy replied, "you're the chief investigator."

...

Will returned from 125 Worth Street with a folder under his arm and wedged himself into my office along with Walter. He had just returned from the two-block journey to the Department of Sanitation's personnel department where he had made copies of our subject's personnel folder, including his photo.

"What do you have?" I asked after the two investigators were as comfortable as they could be in my tiny office space.

Will opened the folder. "Joseph Franchese has been a sanman for 16-years. He's assigned to Queens West 1 and lives in Hicksville, in Nassau County."

"What's his job record like?" I asked.

"Marginal," Will replied. "He's had several minor disciplinary actions against him, and he's been on the sick abuse twice during his career. He also has been out sick for long periods, including now for a back injury that is claimed to be job related."

"How old is he?" I asked.

Will scanned through the papers in the folder. "forty-two."

"Let me see the photo," I said. The black and white head shot looked like it could have come off the wall of an FBI chart depicting a mafia family.

"Okay," I began. "This is gonna be pretty simple to begin the case, and maybe pretty simple to end it."

"What are we gonna do?" Walter asked.

"The allegation is that he has an ownership interest in Atlas Body Shop in Queens Village." I looked at Will. "I assume you already went to the Department of Consumer Affairs and looked up the owner information?"

"I did," Will nodded. "The owner of record is Cosmo Carbone. Franchese's name doesn't appear anywhere on the ownership records."

"That's a good start," I said, but it doesn't close the case. We are going to have to visit the body shop a few times and see if he's there. If we never see him there, we can close the case."

"And if he's there?" Walter asked.

I sighed deeply. "Then, the fun begins."

Queens Village was primarily a quiet, middle class residential neighborhood in eastern Queens, but there was a small section of the area filled with salvage yards and auto body shops. The moment Will turned the car onto the block I had flashbacks from my first day of patrol on Lombardy Street. The entire block was filthy, with tall weeds and garbage strewn along the street and sidewalk providing the atmosphere for the businesses on the block. About halfway down the street was a dirty faded sign attached to an old brick structure that read "Atlas."

Will parked the car about a block and a half from the body shop. Once he had put the vehicle into park, he turned toward the passenger seat. "Okay, now what?"

"Now, we see if he's inside." I said. "Who's going in?"

Walter already had the back door open. "I'll go,"

"You studied the photo, right?" I asked.

"Yeah, yeah," Walter said, "and I know he's six feet tall and 240 pounds."

"Good luck," I said as the back door slammed shut.

Five minutes later Walter jumped into the back seat. "He was in there," he panted.

"Was he working?" I asked.

Walter shook his head. "I don't know."

"Well, what did you do inside the shop?" I asked.

"I asked the guy behind the counter about getting a brake job."

"He was behind the counter?" I inquired.

"No, no," Walter shot back. "Another guy was behind the counter, but I could see through a door into the work area, and he was walking around in there."

"Was he working on a car?" I asked.

Walter shrugged. "I'm not sure. He may have been, but he also could have been checking on the progress of work on his own car – I couldn't tell."

"Why didn't you stay until you could make that determination?" I asked.

"Because the guy behind the counter worked really fast. I asked him how much a brake job would cost for my car, and he gave me a price. I couldn't hang around any longer."

I took off my seatbelt and opened the driver's door. "I'm going in."

"What are you gonna say?" Will asked.

"I'll think of something," I smiled as I slammed the door shut.

As I walked down the block, I decided to walk into the office as a potential customer to inquire about a paint job for my car. The office was small, grimy, and cluttered, everything you would think an urban body shop would be. I approached the chipped wooden counter and attracted the attention of an extremely obese, 30–35-year-old White male who was wearing a black T-shirt with "Go Fuck Yourself" printed on its front.

"Yeah" the employee grumbled, exhibiting excellent customer service.

I started rambling on about my paint job to the complete disinterest of this rotund fellow. As I spoke, I was concentrating on a doorway behind him and to the right that appeared to lead into the working area of the body shop. Seated in a folding chair about ten feet inside this doorway, conversing with a man equally as large as my current partner in conversation, was Joe Franchese. I asked just about every question possible about a paint job, much to the annoyance of my new friend, in order to maintain my vantage point. I finally departed the office with Franchese still visible seated inside the shop. Maybe he was having work done on a car. Maybe he just stopped to talk to a friend. Maybe it was any of a hundred other explanations. The point was, however, this case could not be closed. In fact, it was just beginning.

"He seems to be more than a customer," I said as I slid back into the passenger's seat.

"What do we do now?" Walter asked.

"We aren't doing anything. You gentlemen are going to conduct a 'lifestyle,'" I said, using a term I picked up in reading the old case folders.

"What's a lifestyle?" Will asked.

"You maintain surveillance on our subject for a period of time."

"How long a period?" Walter asked.

I stroked my chin. "Hmm, let's see. I think a week would be good."

"And what do we do for a week?" Will followed up.

"You see where he goes and what he does," I explained. "In other words, you develop what his lifestyle is."

"What's that going to accomplish?" Walter asked.

"I'm not sure now," I replied. "We'll meet in a week to see what you have and then we'll determine what the next step will be."

...

"It may not be clear if he works or owns that body shop," Will said, "but one thing is clear."

"What?" I asked.

"Joe Franchese loves the ladies."

"Isn't he married?" I asked.

"Sure," Will nodded, "with two teenage girls. What difference does that make?"

"Silly me," I shrugged. "So, what makes you think he's a Don Juan?"

"Well," Will began, "except for visiting the body shop for a few minutes on three occasions, there was one place he spent hours at every evening."

"Where?"

"That new Jack LaLane Fitness Club that opened in East Meadow."

"That's odd," I said. "When I saw him inside the body shop he didn't look like the exercising type. As a matter of fact, he looked like he was substantially overweight."

"He is," Walter answered, 'but he doesn't spend much time in the club working out."

"What do you mean?" I asked.

"The club is in a shopping center," Will said, "so we were able to park outside the club with a great view through the huge glass window."

"We also went inside," Walter said. "The club offered a free tour and workout, so both of us went in on different days while Franchese was inside."

"Yeah," Will groaned. "I'm still stiff."

I was growing impatient. "What about Don Juan?"

"You should see this guy work," Walter grinned. "He's got this charming smile, a line for every lady, and a charisma that seems to draw women to him like moths to a flame."

"Sounds like you like him?" I chuckled.

"Very funny, Chief." Walter frowned.

Will continued before any other comments could be made. "He really seemed to love the attention he received from women. It was like he enjoyed the thrill of the chase – always on the prowl for his next conquest."

"Was he successful?" I asked.

"His success is in his confidence," Walter explained. "He threw his line in the water so many times that it would be almost impossible for him not to hook a fish every now and then."

I placed my hands behind my head and leaned back in mt chair. "So, you took a week to determine our subject is a snake in the grass. The question is – what are we going to do with this information?"

Will cleared his throat. "I have an idea, Chief."

"Well, don't keep it to yourself," I said.

Will began, "This gentleman seems to fancy himself a swordsman, correct?"

Walter and I nodded.

"So, why don't we use the weapon that has been most effective throughout recorded civilization."

Walter and I stared at Will, and he stared back. Finally, with a look indicating that he never thought he would have to explain further, he blurted, "A woman!"

"What about a woman?" I asked.

"My plan," Will explained, "will be to arrange a chance encounter between Franchese and a female, who would be playing the role of a helpless female motorist in a disabled car. This set up should not be difficult because we know where his pickup truck is parked just about every evening – in the parking lot near the health club. The only tricky part of the plan would be to get the female's car parked very close to Franchese's vehicle, and then disable it in some way so that the engine would not turn over. As Franchese would be walking to his truck, he would pass right by our lady in distress, and hopefully chivalry would rule the day, and he would stop to help her. Once engaged, our girl would expound on a theme that she had the car for less than a year and that it was nothing but trouble. She would go on to say that she was sick of the car and that she wished she could just get rid of it, but that no one in their right mind would buy it, considering all its issues. The goal of the pretext was to get Franchese so enamored with our girl that he would use his connection with the body shop to at minimum offer to do some work on the car for a minimal price or at best offer to do an "insurance job" on her car."

"Who said anything about an insurance job?" I asked.

"Come on, Chief," Will grinned, "A lot of these Queens body shops are shady. I'm just speculating."

"I don't know about speculating," I said, "but in actuality, it's not a bad idea."

"Thanks," Will smiled.

"There's only one problem," I noted.

"What's that?" Will asked.

"Where do we find a woman?"

"Why not use Liz?" Will shot back.

"That's not much of a woman?" Walter snickered.

I tried to select my words carefully. I didn't want to send the message that I was saying Liz was better than nothing, so I simply said, "She'll do, if she's willing."

"Liz!" I yelled loud enough to be heard in the investigator's room.

Within a few seconds she appeared at my doorway. "Yes, chief."

"Try to jam another chair in here. There's something I want to go over with you."

Once Liz had wedged her way into my office I laid the entire scenario out for her, and what her role would be. "This is going above and beyond," I added, "so I would never force you do it. It's your choice if you're comfortable with it."

Liz didn't miss a beat. "I'd love to do it," She chirped.

"Good," I nodded. "Now we just have to figure out a car."

"No problem," Liz gushed, "we can use my car."

"Okay, then," I shrugged. "I'll bring Greg on board, and we'll meet tomorrow evening at 5:00 P.M. near the health club and go over the specifics of the operation." I looked to my left. "Will is gonna let us know specifically where in the area we'll meet."

...

At 5:05 P.M. the next evening I sat with Walter, Will, Greg and Liz in a small coffee shop across from the shopping center where the Jack LaLane Health Club was located. Will was talking about Franchese's usual activities in and around the health club, but I was mesmerized by the chair to Will's right. I had only seen plain homely Liz in the drab, conservative business attire she wore to the office. Now, she was dressed for an evening of socializing, and she looked like a completely different person – she was perfect. I was looking at a very petite female with long, straight dark hair accentuated by piercing dark eyes. She was still far from drop dead gorgeous, but her wholesome pleasant nature was irresistible. Above all, her pretty, but not knock out, soccer mom MILF looks should make her seem obtainable to a self-absorbed Romeo like Joe Franchese.

I had found a book in the office about undercover operations, so I decided to utilize the terminology I had read about. "This operation will involve one UC and four ghosts."

"Could you please repeat that in English?" Greg asked.

"Liz is the undercover while the rest of us are ghosts, meaning that we will keep surveillance on Liz without being seen."

"Why didn't you say that in the first place?" Joe grunted.

I bit my lip and continued with the assignments. "The ghost assignments are Walter and Will in Will's car and me and Greg in my car."

"How am I going to get in place?" Liz asked.

"Greg, me and you will hang out in the far corner of the parking lot." I explained. "Walter and Will are going to get close to the health club and as soon as they see where he parks, we'll hopefully be able to get you as close as possible to his pickup."

"How are we gonna communicate?" Walter asked.

"With these," I said, holding up two walkie talkie radios. "I found these in the office supply closet, and they seem to work fine. I'll keep one in my car and Will and Walter will keep the other one. When you see Franchese park call me on the radio, and I'll tell Liz to move up and park where you tell her to."

"I would just like to go over my role bryan, Chief," Liz said.

"Sure," I nodded. "You're a female in distress standing outside your disabled vehicle. You look very flustered not knowing what to do. When Franchese walks by wait to see if he engages with you, and if not, you ask if maybe he could help you."

"And my endgame is…" Liz asked.

"All you want to do is to have him tell you to bring the car to his shop so he can look at it."

"What if I'm not comfortable with how things are going?"

"The moment you feel uncomfortable," I explained, "you tell him that you already called your brother on a payphone, and he will be here any minute. When I see you take off that cute hat you're wearing, that will be my cue to come on the scene."

"Okay," Liz replied, "I guess we have everything covered."

"One thing," Will remarked. "How are we disabling Liz's car."

I grit my teeth and took a long deep breath. I had thought of everything but the obvious. Before I could try to think of a solution, Greg jumped to the rescue. "It's easy, Chiefy. My partner has a new Honda. They all have a fuel shut off valve in the trunk. As soon as she gets parked, I'll just open the trunk and close the valve. With that valve closed the engine won't start."

"That's great," I said, "but what if Franchese knows that too. If he looks in the trunk, he'll see the valve is closed."

"So,what?" Greg shrugged. "Liz can tell him she was moving things around in the trunk and must have hit the valve. If that happens, he's still the hero for discovering it."

"Sounds good," I said. "Okay, Walter and Will, get as close to the gym as you can, and we'll drive over to the far corner of the parking lot. I'll wait a few minutes to let you get into position and then do a radio check."

I learned something about Greg while sitting in my car with him for two hours. Much to my chagrin, I learned he was an opera fan, and to pass the time he enjoyed singing opera, and not singing very well.

"Does that song ever end?" I groaned.

"What's the matter, Chiefy," Greg smiled, "I'm just exposing you to some culture."

I shook my head. "You should be singing solo – so low I can't hear you!"

"That's pretty good," Greg chuckled, before he burst into his next off-key selection.

Salvation finally arrived in the form of static followed by Walter's voice on the walkie talkie. "He's here, and we scored bigtime."

"Repeat that," I said into my radio.

"He parked and the space directly to his left was open," Walter replied. "We pulled into the space. As soon as Liz gets up here, we'll pull out and let her in"

"10-4," I said. I turned to Greg. "I'm gonna jump out and let Liz know." I trotted up to Liz's driver's side window. "Will and Walter are holding a space for you up near the gym directly next to Franchese's pickup truck. When you get up there, they'll pull out and let you pull in."

"Got it, Chief."

Once Liz was parked, Greg managed to pull his bulk out of my car. He looked at Franchese's pick up and nodded, "Nice truck."

Liz stood at her open trunk while I implored Greg to stay focused. "Forget about his truck, just take care of the fuel valve."

"You got it, Chiefy," Greg said.

Five minutes later, our final plan was in place. Will and Walter were parked in the first row of spaces where they had a clear view of the gym door. When they observed Franchese leave the gym Walter would notify me on the radio. Liz and Franchese were in the third row of parking spaces and my car was in the fourth row, directly behind Liz's car. Once I received the radio call that Franchese was on the move, I would flash my bright lights which would be the signal for Liz to get out of her car, open the hood, and look as helpless as possible. We were set.

At 10:05 PM I had endured horrible renditions of Carmen, The Barber of Seville, and The Marriage of Figaro when mercifully, Walter's voice crackled over the radio. "Subject exiting the gym."

I flashed the bright lights causing Liz to exit her car and raise the hood. She then re-entered her car and began unsuccessfully attempting to start the engine. I didn't think she was going to stay in the car, but her timing turned out to be perfect.

As Franchese passed by the rear of Liz's vehicle, she was still unsuccessfully trying to start the car. It was obvious that Franchese noticed the problem because he visibly slowed down as he approached the driver's door of his truck. Liz then popped out of the car looking every inch the flustered, helpless female. With the new and improved version of Liz prancing helplessly around her vehicle, it took Franchese all of about 30-seconds to take the bait. In the quiet night air with my window rolled down, I could clearly hear Franchese at work.

"Having a problem, miss?" Franchese sank his teeth deep into the hook and Liz began to methodically reel him in.

She was a fantastic combination of frustration, anger and fear, and at just the right moments a little bit of flirtation would come through. The conversation progressed exactly as planned with Liz vocalizing her disgust for the vehicle that had become a money pit for her. Franchese, for his part, handled the situation like a true snake. Through his shallow attempts to determine where Liz would seek assistance, he quickly established that she had neither a husband nor a boyfriend. I could hear Liz loud and clear as the conversation reached a conflict for the first time. Franchese was turning purely social and was attempting to obtain Liz's phone number and to make a date. Liz was entertaining the social banter while still trying to turn the conversation back to her car problems. I winced when I heard Liz give him her real phone number and they talked about getting together over the weekend. The conversation was beginning to drag, and I was hoping Liz's hat would come off soon so that her brother could arrive on the scene. Without warning, it was Franchese who took the game to the next level.

"You have fire and theft?" he asked.

"Sure," Liz responded in a puzzled voice.

Franchese laid it out. "If you want, I can take this for you now."

"What do you mean?" Liz continued her bewilderment.

"I'll call my shop and a tow will be here in 20-minutes to tow it in. Problem solved."

Did I just hear him correctly? Was he offering to do the insurance job right now? I thought I had planned for every possible exigency that could develop in this operation, but I had not considered that 20-minutes after he met Liz, he would offer to get rid of the car. For a moment panic set in as I considered how to respond to the offer.

Greg upped my fears when he turned to me with a little smile and said, "If she goes through with this, I wonder if she realizes shell get her car back in little pieces."

It finally occurred to me that I could not let Franchese take the car. Greg was right. Once that car was inside the body shop it would be chopped to pieces and there would be nothing we could do about it. But there was also a more important reason for me to abort the operation. If her car was being towed, Liz would have to ride alone with Franchese in his tuck. I never planned for any alone time with the two potential lovebirds, and I did not want to put Liz in that position without her prior consent. I quickly turned to Greg and said, "Time for the brother to appear."

The instant I walked up I could detect Franchese's disappointment when Liz introduced me as the brother she had previously called from the payphone. I went right to her trunk and told her to open it. "Were you fooling around in here with anything?" I asked.

Liz played along. "I needed to make room for packages, so I moved a lot of my junk to one side."

"Of course," I said. "You accidentally turned off the gas flow valve." I flipped the valve. "It will start now."

Liz continued her outstanding performance. She thanked Franchese for his help, but I was stunned when she said that she hoped they could get together over the weekend. Her parting shot was saying that she still hoped that he could help her do something with her car.

Once Franchese had departed the parking lot, the team reassembled in the coffee shop across the street. "That was great, Liz," I said, but I shook my head. "I didn't count on you giving him your phone number and going out on a date with him."

"Why not?" Liz asked. "I'm a big girl. I can take care of myself and I'm up for the challenge."

"I don't know," I pondered. "It may be a moot point, anyway. He may not call."

"Don't worry about that," Liz chuckled. "I know men, and this guy will call."

"I think we should do it, Chief," Will said, while Walter nodded in agreement.

"What do you think, Greg?" I asked.

"Why not?" he shrugged. "I'll get a chance to sing to you some more."

I rolled my eyes. "I can't wait," I took a sip of soda. "Okay, if he calls, we'll work out a plan. Just make sure you make the date for someplace that's active, but somewhere we can park our cars close by."

...

Liz turned out to be correct and she also followed my directions. Franschese did call and they arranged to meet on Saturday evening for dinner and drinks in the Bayside section of Queens. The restaurant agreed upon was the First Edition located on Bell Blvd. in a section known as the Miracle Mile due to the propensity of bars and restaurants.

The vehicle assignments were the same as the previous operation, except that Walter and Will were going to be inside the restaurant where they could always maintain observation of Liz. There were two other arrangements I made through Andy. He was able to contact the department of investigation and receive petty cash for the evening. I knew I would have to issue cash to Will and Walter, but I hoped Franchese was at least enough of a gentleman to pay for Liz's meal. The other arrangement Andy made with DOI was to receive the use of a Kel for the night. A Kel was a small recording device that Liz could wear for the evening. I was stuck once again sitting in my car listening to the off-key opera.

Liz was to meet Franchese outside the restaurant, and once Will and Walter observed Liz and her date enter, they would also enter for an enjoyable dinner at a table where they could maintain eyes on Sandy.

Franchese was late as Liz paced back in forth in front of the restaurant. I was being tortured by Greg's rendition of Rigoletto when I thought I saw John Travolta, in his Saturday Night Fever wardrobe striding down Bell Blvd, only this Travolta had gained a lot of weight. Liz provided an obligatory peck on the cheek as the couple disappeared behind the large wooden door. Game on.

Once they were seated Will excused himself to use the restroom, but instead came outside to tell me that they were seated several tables away, and they had good eyes on Liz. There was nothing left for me except to listen to Greg's atrocious voice. Suddenly, a light bulb appeared above my head, and I ran across the street, returning with two dozen Dunkin Donuts. That should stop him from singing for at least 30-minutes.

Walter came outside during one of his bathroom visits and said that the date appeared to be wrapping up. He also said that Franchese had been drinking heavily during the evening and seemed to be coming on aggressively to Liz.

I was now worried, and I was elated that Liz had found a parking space almost directly in front of the restaurant, so she didn't have to walk down a dark, residential street with this Casanova. I punched Greg on the arm as he was working on a refill of donuts I had provided. "There they are," I declared.

Liz was taking no chances, as she playfully was avoiding his gropes, trying to look as if she was enjoying the cat and mouse game. She arrived at her driver's door and was inside before Franchese knew what happened. Liz was professional enough to know that she could not just drive off, so she sat in her driver's seat with the window open while Franchese appeared to be trying to fit his entire body through the window. Liz had to surrender several brief kisses, but suddenly the driver's window was up, and the car was on the move. As Liz's vehicle disappeared into the night Joe Franchese stood alone in the vacated parking space. I pictured the scene as a still photo with the caption "Most disappointed man in New York".

Liz was already waiting in the municipal parking lot when I pulled into the space next to her. Two minutes later Will and Walter joined us, and we all adjourned to the coffee shop across the street.

Liz handed me the Kel. "That was an experience," she smirked.

"I guess it wasn't the best date you've ever been on," I grinned.

"Not quite," Liz replied," but there's some interesting stuff on that tape."

"Tell us about how he acted on the date first," I said.

"Yeah," Walter added, "From our vantage point he just looked sleazy."

"Okay," Liz sighed. "From the time we were seated at the table he seemed tense and agitated. He was snapping at the waiter and was visibly irritated by the noise in the restaurant. I even tried to make small talk, but his responses were short and curt."

"Sounds like a nice guy," Will remarked.

"When the food arrived," Liz continued, "he complained about the taste and texture of the dish and demanded that the waiter bring him a new dish."

"It doesn't seem like a very fun date," I said.

"Are you kidding?" Liz gasped. "That was the best part of the night. Things only got worse from there. He began criticizing my clothes and appearance. He said my outfit wasn't sexy enough and that I should have worn something more revealing. Every time I tried to steer the conversation to my car, he would always say, 'I'll take care of you if you take care of me.'"

"What a great line," Greg snickered.

"I think everything else that happened is better explained in the tape," Liz said.

I placed the recorder in the middle of the table and pressed "play." I breathed a sigh of relief when it was clear from the start that the audio was good, with Franchese's voice completely understandable.

As the tape progressed it was clear that I had not considered the depths of Franchese's degeneracy. Throughout the entire night, his end of the conversation was filled with sexual innuendos and double entendre comments, with some outright propositions sprinkled in. At one point, Franchese proudly mentioned that his nickname was the tripod. Liz must have had a puzzled look on her face because he immediately explained how a tripod has three legs, and how the length of one of his appendages made him tripod-like. Combined with the groping that Walter and Will witnessed, along with his attempt at a final make out session through her car window, I completely understood why Liz wanted no part of another meeting with Don Juan.

There were tales of sexual prowess throughout the tape, but finally, we did start hearing the more pertinent information. As Liz skillfully led him to the subject of the body shop, Franchese finally got to the "good stuff."

Franchese detailed how he became "involved" with the collision and body shop business several years earlier. He stated that a couple of days after he was in the business, he was visited at the shop by two guys who looked like they jumped right out of the Godfather movie. He continued to relate how these two large gentlemen said that they represented a private carting service, and they inquired as to what days of the week he would like pick-ups. Franchese said that he politely informed the gentlemen that he already had a carter and that their services were not required at this time, to which one of the behemoths calmly handed him a small piece of paper with a phone number and said to call him when he changed his mind. Franchese said that he found it odd that he had said "when" you change your mind, as opposed to "if" you change your mind. Franchese continued that about two hours after this meeting he was sitting alone inside the shop office looking over some paperwork, when the silence of the moment was interrupted by automatic gunfire. He said that he instinctually hit the deck as the glass office window appeared to disintegrate in the explosions. He heard the sound of tires screeching as the gunfire ended, followed by a return to silence. Franchese stated that when he perceived the danger had passed, he got up and surveyed the scene to find the office window completely gone and the front of the body shop riddled with bullet holes. He said that he immediately pulled out the small piece of paper from his pants pocket, dialed the number from his office phone, and said Monday's Wednesday's and Friday's would be fine for pick-ups.

Everyone at the table agreed that the story surely qualified as "good stuff," but there was more. There were several stories of making cars disappear, but the stories lacked a lot of detail. This lack of detail wasn't Liz's fault. Every time it seemed that she was about to get into some specific information about the operations of the body shop and his specific association, Franchese's loins interrupted, and we were off and running with a new string of amorous lines.

At the conclusion of the tape, I realized we had reached the end of the road. I was frustrated because the tape clearly convinced me that Franchese was hooked up with the shady activities at the body shop, but all his verbal admissions were vague enough that I questioned if they were actually of any value.

...

Monday morning, I sat inside Andy's office listening to Franchese's rantings for a second time. The button on the recorder popped up and the office became silent.

"What do you think?" I asked.

"There's nothing there to go to DOI with criminally." Andy said.

"That's what I figured," I agreed.

"But," Andy continued, "There's plenty there to go after him departmentally."

"Really?"

"Sure," Andy said. "We'll call him down to the department trial room at Worth Street where he can be formally questioned. After that interview we can initiate formal department charges against him." Andy smiled. "With or without the shady body shop dealings, we have him cold being out of his residence numerous times while out sick."

"I guess you're right," I nodded. "Who will conduct the interview?"

"You will," Andy replied.

"Me?"

"Why not?" Andy shrugged. "It's your case. I'll call to book the trial room and to make the notification for him to appear Wednesday morning. It will give you a day to prep."

"Gee, thanks," I groaned.

...

Joe Franchese entered the trial room in full uniform accompanied by his short, chunky union attorney. As Franchese settled into the chair opposite me, I was able to finally get a good look at him. He was 42 years old, but his trendy hairstyle and tan told me that he was working hard to appear 32. I detected a mixture of puzzlement and disgust on his face. Disgust at having to deal with the rats from the IG's office and puzzlement at not knowing why he was being interviewed.

Since the operation had been Will's idea, I brought him with me to assist with the questioning. Sanitation men have to file paperwork with the department stating they are working a part time job, so I let Will begin with a preliminary, but very important question that would set the stage for the remainder of the interview.

"Do you have any current authorized off duty employment?" Will asked.

"No." was Franchese's response.

Will continued, " Have you ever heard of Atlas Collision?"

Franchese shrugged his shoulders. "Yeah."

I took over the questioning. "What's your association with Atlas?"

Franchese: "I don't have an association."

Murphy: "You've never been there?"

Franchese: "Yeah, I've been there."

Murphy: "For what purpose?"

Franchese: "For the purpose that most people go to a body shop"

Murphy: "And what reason might that be?"

Franchese: "To have work done on my car."

Murphy: "Have you gone to Atlas for work more than once?"

Franchese: "I've been there lots of times. What's your point?"

Murphy: "At ease, Mr. Franchese. Just answer the questions"

Franchese: "I can't tell you exactly how many times I've been there, but I've had work done there on my last three cars."

Murphy: "Do you know the owner of Atlas?

Franchese: "Yeah"

Murphy: "What's his name?"

Franchese: "Joe"

Murphy: "Joe what?"

Vigoda: "I don't know, but it's not Joe Franchese if that's what you're asking?"

Murphy: "Have you ever worked at Atlas?"

Franchese: "Are you serious?"

Murphy: " Have you ever worked at Atlas?"

Franchese: "No"

Murphy: "Do you have any ownership interest in Atlas?"

Franchese: "This is ridiculous"

Murphy: " This is your last warning, sir. Answer the question."

Franchese: "No"

Murphy: "During anytime that you were present at Atlas, did you ever witness or participate in any criminal activity

Franchese was more subdued, "No."

I produced the tape recorder and stated, "I have something I would like you to listen to Mr. Franchese."

I did not wait for a response as I pressed "play". I studied Franchese's face for some clue as to the emotions he was feeling. I detected curiosity, bewilderment, and a little arrogance, but by far the most prominent emotion coming through was disappointment when the reality set in that Liz had not been a typical female who had fallen for his masculine perfection.

The tape wound its way through the automatic gunfire, the admissions of owning a body shop, and the magical act of making cars disappear on demand. When the recording concluding, the depressed play button automatically snapped up with a pop. There was a brief silence until Franchese looked at me and said, "You set me up, huh."

The look on his face was a little strange as I could almost detect some admiration in the fact that we had been able to fool a genius such as himself.

I began to bring the questioning home. "You said that you have no association with Atlas, and that you have never witnessed or participated in criminal activities there. How do you explain your statements on this tape?"

Franchese leaned back in his chair and tilted his head slightly to the right. He appeared to be deep in thought. Finally, he took a very deep breath and placed his hands in the air in the surrender position. "What do you want me to say Lieutenant. I meet a girl and I become a bullshit artist. Sometimes I tell her I own an ice cream parlor. Sometimes I tell her I'm a cowboy, and sometimes I tell her I own a body shop. What do you want from me. I'll say anything to get into a girl's pants."

As crude and classless as this answer was, it was also effective, and based on the smug look on his face, he realized that we had nowhere else to go with this.

Well, at least I could finish up by wiping that smug look off his face. "Have you received permission from the sick desk to be out of your residence every time you visited the Jack LaLane Health Club?"

The expression on his face transformed from smug to "Oh Shit". I have to admit I enjoyed dragging him through the details of every day that he was working out at the gym while he was out sick with his back injury. And just like that, the case was over. Franchese received a thirty-day suspension and a year's dismissal probation and we moved on to new investigations.

CHAPTER 13:

The next two years flew by. My unit had become a very tight knit group who I enjoyed managing very much. I even became used to Greg's horrendous singing. With each case my crew and myself improved our investigative skills until most of the work became very routine.

The only problem I had with working in the IG's office was my old man. From the first day I told him about the assignment two years earlier, he was aghast that his son would be working for the rat squad. My dad had always taken a keen interest in my activities, and he was thrilled when I joined the Sanitation Department, and very proud when I became a Sanitation Police Officer. But he hadn't said a word to me about my job since I joined the Inspector General's office.

It was another day at the office. I sat at my desk and studied the current caseload. All the cases were up to date and all the closed cases forwarded to DOI had been approved. I had done it. Somehow, in two years I had convinced these kids just out of college that I knew what I was talking about regarding investigations and turned them into effective investigators. I felt so good that I rewarded myself on this morning with a few moments to take a break and read the newspaper.

"I see you're busy," Andy chuckled from my office doorway.

"You may not believe this," I said, "but this is the first time since we took over this office that I have stopped to read the paper."

"You're right, I don't believe it," Andy laughed. "Actually," he continued, "you've done a fantastic job, and that makes it all the more difficult to carry this news."

"What news?" I gulped.

"I just spoke with the Sanitation Commissioner and the Commissioner of DOI. They both think you're doing a great job too."

"I sense a 'but' coming," I said.

"But – they decided that the inspector general's office should not have uniformed personnel. They want the investigative staff to be all civilians."

"Why?"

"They think there will be less chance of civilians showing favoritism to employees, since they never worked in the field with them."

"That's ridiculous," I grumbled.

"I know," Andy shrugged, "but I'm sorry – that's the way it is."

"I know it's not your fault, Andy." I stood and approached my office door with my hand extended. "It's been a pleasure working with you."

"The feeling is mutual," Andy nodded as we shook hands.

When we released hands, I returned to the chair behind my desk. "My only question is what am I supposed to do now?"

"Call Inspector Malloy," Andy directed. "He'll have the details of your next assignment."

"Hello Inspector, It's Jim Murphy."

"Hello, Jim, I'm sorry this happened to you, but this is what the commissioner wants."

"It is what it is, Inspector," I sighed. "No use crying about it."

"Still, it's a shame, especially when I heard what a good job you were doing."

"I guess things could be worse," I chuckled.

"How so?"

"I get the feeling you're getting ready to tell me I'm no longer a lieutenant."

"No way," Malloy roared. "I would never do that to you."

"That's good to hear, Inspector."

"I'm putting you in charge of Queens," Malloy said.

"Really?" I gushed.

"Hold on, Jimmy Boy," Malloy cautioned. "Before you get too excited, we're only talking about a handful of cops. On a daily basis there will probably be three or four sanitation cops for you to supervise throughout the entire borough."

"How do I supervise them?"

"Just visit them when they're on patrol and sign their memo books," Malloy said. "Make sure they are out there doing their jobs and not sitting in the back of some bar."

"Sounds complicated," I scoffed.

"That's all I have for you right now. In a few months, something may open up where I can put you in charge of a plainclothes squad working illegal dumping. But for now, go out there and show the flag on the streets of Queens. At least I'll make sure you have an unmarked car available for your use."

"Thanks."

...

On most days, my supervisory patrol in Queens involved keeping tabs on only three cops. On a Tuesday approximately two weeks into the assignment, I had one cop assigned to the Astoria / Long Island City area. The second was focusing his efforts in Jamaica, and the third was patrolling in Jackson Heights and Corona. I had already visited two cops and signed their memo books, and I was driving to my third rendezvous. I called the cop over the radio and discovered he was working currently in Corona on 105th Street. I told him to wait there for my arrival.

I turned down 103rd street three blocks south of Roosevelt Avenue. About 300-feet before the intersection with Roosevelt Avenue I came to a stop so suddenly that the car behind me came dangerously close to slamming into my rear bumper. I didn't hear the blaring horn or curses as the irate motorist passed me. I was too focused on something I had seen on the right side of the road. It was a sign that read "Variety Store." It was the same store where the creeps had torn up my summons, motivating me to issue two more. I scanned the sidewalk in front of the store which was at least as filthy, if not dirtier than it had been during my previous visit. I parked and exited my vehicle.

The sidewalk on 103rd Street was filled with its usual high volume of pedestrian traffic as I weaved my way across the sidewalk, sidestepping human traffic and garbage along the way. The bell attached to the door rang announcing my entrance into the variety store. The older Middle Eastern man came out of the back room. I did not see the younger man or anyone else in the store.

The older man smiled as he approached, but he seemed extremely nervous. "How may I assist you, Mr. Officer?"

I pointed to the front door. "Your sidewalk is dirtier than it was the last time I was here."

The man placed his hands together and bowed. "So sorry Mr. Officer. I will sweep."

"When will you sweep?" I asked.

"Later," He pointed to the back room. "Very busy with inventory right now."

I noticed we were not alone anymore. At the far end of the main aisle, I could see the younger male standing in the doorway to the back room.

The older man walked past me and motioned for me to follow him to the front. "Show me what exactly what you want me to clean, Mr. Officer."

I turned toward the front door and took two steps. "It's not as case of what I want you to clean. The whole sidewalk is filthy."

I remember something that felt like an electric shock going through the back of my head before everything went black.

When I woke up the first thought to enter my mind was how small the room was. The next thought was to wonder where I was, followed by the realization that my hands were bound in front of me. Very quickly, I became aware of more facts. My police shirt, shield and bullet proof vest had been removed along with my gun belt. I was sitting in my white t-shirt and blue police pants with my hands tied in front of me. Adding to my cramped feeling was the fact that I was the fourth person inside these small quarters, which I was reasonably sure was the back room of the variety store. The older and younger creep were present along with another middle eastern younger creep. They probably thought I was still unconscious as they spoke in something resembling English that I could mostly understand. I was scared and the conversation I heard only served to increase my fear.

"Welcome brother," the older creep said to the new creep. "This is a great day. It is the day of our great operation."

All the creeps began a chorus of "God is great" The older creep placed his hand on the new creep's shoulder and continued his speech. "Today, our brother Marwan becomes a hero of the jihad."

With my head still pounding, I was trying to digest what was going on, and my keen investigative instincts told me nothing good was happening, especially when I took a close look at the creep called Marwan. The two original creeps had unkempt hair and long beards, but Marwan was clean shaven with closely cropped hair. This was an unsettling red flag for me. I had just been to a training course given by the NYPD where the instructor said that Muslims traditionally purify corpses by washing the skin and nails and sometimes by shaving the pubic hair. But suicide attackers are deprived of a proper burial since there are usually no remains. To compensate, the instructor said the attackers shear themselves ahead of time, both to guarantee some level of cleanliness at the time of instant incineration and to prove extreme devotion to personal purity. I gulped as I noted how clean Marwan looked for what could be his appointment in heaven. Any doubts about Marwan's intent were dashed as I continued to study the clean-shaven creep. The vest Marwan was wearing made my eyes widen. That's a bomb vest, I thought.

The situation went from bad to worse when the older creep, who Marwan called Waheed, wheeled forward a green backpack/duffel bag.

"What's in the backpack?" Marwan queried.

"A grand gift from God," Waheed happily responded.

I was stumped. If creepy Marwan was already wearing the bomb, what great gift could God have put in the backpack? Further thought on the backpack would have to wait as Waheed continued to talk about the operation.

"Marwan, my brother, you will ride the subway into Manhattan. Once at Times Square you will detonate the bomb in your vest and God willing, that explosion will bring forth the great gift." Waheed raised his hands in praise. "With God's grace, every infidel in Manhattan will be sacrificed."

I quickly switched gears from worrying about New York City to worrying about my life. Obviously, there was no way these creeps could leave me alive to tell the story. The ropes binding my hands were tight, but there was a slight bit of play in them. I began slowly rotating my hands and wrists in an attempt to begin the loosening process without drawing attention to myself.

Waheed's smile was gone as he slapped my already throbbing head. "So, you're awake."

"He heard the entire plan," the original young creep fumed.

Waheed's smile returned. "It doesn't matter, Rashid. He's not going to tell anyone."

My brains must have still been rattled, because at that moment, for some absurd reason, I believed an attempt at humor was in order. "I have an important appointment, and I can't be late, so you fellas will have to go on without me."

"Shut up!" Again, my head ached from a sharp blow to the back of my head by the young creep named Rashid.

I took a deep breath and tried to convince myself of the importance of remaining calm. If I was not calm, I may not recognize an opportunity to escape if it ever materialized.

Waheed grabbed me by the arm and yanked me to my feet. I could see through the open back door through to the front of the store. Rashid had locked the door and placed a CLOSED sign on the front door. At least the conditions were no longer cramped as Waheed pulled me onto the selling floor.

Waheed addressed the group and went over the operational plan. The simplest part of the operation was the route and destination. Marwan would be taken to the Willets Point elevated subway station where he would board a 7-train and ride into Times Square. If no problems developed, he would carry his backpack up to the street, detonate his vest, and whatever great gift was inside the backpack. If at any time during the train ride he sensed a problem, Marwan was to detonate his bomb immediately. The most difficult part of the tactics involved getting Marwan familiar with the trigger to his bomb vest. Waheed explained that it was a pressure trigger.

Marwan would hold the trigger in his hand and squeeze it. Once the trigger was armed, the moment Marwan released the pressure on the trigger, the bomb would detonate. It was actually a very simple trigger, but I could sense Waheed's apprehension. Obviously, I was not alone in my opinion that creepy Marwan was also stupid Marwan.

For a good fifteen minutes Waheed made Marwan hold a hand grip exerciser. He would instruct Marwan to squeeze the grip and hold it tight. At some point he would tell Marwan to release his grip. At the moment Marwan released the grip, Waheed would shout "BOOM". Finally, Waheed was confident that even a simpleton like Marwan understood the pressure trigger. I was becoming frantic. During Marwan's fifteen minutes of pressure trigger training, the pressure on me continued to mount. I had no idea what to do to summon help, and I had only slightly managed to loosen the ropes binding my hands.

Waheed nodded and Rashid left the store. Five minutes later I heard three short blasts of a car horn emanating from outside the store.

The horn stirred Waheed to action. "Let's go," he said to Marwan while yanking me by the arm to the door.

Waheed maintained a tight grip on my arm and used his body to shield the fact that my hands were tied. He pushed me into the back seat of a beat-up Toyota Camry parked in front and pushed me across the seat to the driver's side of the vehicle. A million thoughts were racing through my brain as Rashid and Marwan deposited the backpack in the trunk. Should I scream? My options became a moot point as I remained frozen as Rashid and Marwan entered the front seat and the car pulled away from the curb. Now that we were out of public view, I noticed that Waheed was holding a pistol near his waist, its barrel pointing upward towards my head.

Rashid pulled the Toyota to a stop on Roosevelt Avenue, adjacent to the stairway of the Willets Point elevated subway station. I noted the same stupid look on Marwan's face as he took his backpack from the trunk and headed towards the station stairs with Rashid providing an escort.

"God is great." Waheed yelled out the rear window to him as he disappeared up the stairs. I was starting to panic. At some point I was going to have to do something, even if it meant doing battle with two armed men in the cramped quarters of the Toyota. I continued working on loosening the ropes.

Rashid returned to the driver's seat. "The device is armed and he's on his way." he said without turning around.

"Good," Waheed responded. "Go to the next stop."

The Toyota pulled away from the curb with me trying to figure out what I was going to do.

"Where are we going now?" I asked.

I did not like the cold emotionless manner in which Waheed responded. "Patience, brother. You'll know soon enough."

Within two minutes I was staring at what could be best described as a post-apocalyptic landscape. What made the environment more surreal was that fact that Shea Stadium, the home of the New York Mets, was plainly visible to the west. The street being traversed by the Toyota was unpaved and full of holes.

Besides being an elevated subway station, Willets Point was also a section of Queens known locally as the Iron Triangle, due to its concentration of auto repair shops, scrapyards, waste processing sites, and similar small industrial businesses. There were no sidewalks or sewers and due to the area's geography and the lack of paved roads, flooding was common during heavy rains. I bounced continually in the back seat, and on two occasions the bump was so severe that I struck my head on the roof of the car.

The scenery of dilapidated junk yards and auto body shops began to thin. My fear level was off the charts when the Toyota came to a stop. We were on a street completely devoid of people, vehicles, and buildings. Both sides of the unpaved dirt road were lined by weeds that were at least four feet high. I gulped as I scanned the surrounding landscape. It did not take a genius to realize this was the perfect location to dump a body. I could feel the perspiration building on my forehead. Suddenly, the perspiration was gone, flying off my forehead from the force of the blows Waheed was raining down on my head.

I tried to fend of the blows, but Waheed pinned my hands down in his lap while Rashid, who had exited the car and opened the rear door, continued to land blows to my head with his 9mm semi-automatic pistol. I was straining to remain conscious as I heard Waheed direct his brother to stop the attack. I felt a little more play in my bound hands. I was getting close to being able to slip out of the rope, but would there be enough time? I felt another sharp blow to my face as I was roughly pushed forward, slamming my face into the rear of the front seat.

"Frisk him." Waheed directed Rashid.

When Rashid had finished his rear search, he threw me back into my original position and completed the frisk to the front of my body. Waheed then forecast the future of New York City and me.

"Today, brother, many thousands of infidels will die, and you, Mr. cleanliness cop will be the first to perish."

Maybe the blows to the head had knocked the fear and panic out of me, but at that moment, seconds away from my own demise, my mind was completely clear. I was wondering if they were going to shoot me in the back seat or march me into the weeds before executing me. I gave one last great pull of my hands against the ropes and my right hand slid out from under the rope, but I kept my hands close together so as not to reveal I was free from the ropes.

Rashid had left the driver's side rear door open. Either they were going to take me out to the weeds or Waheed was simply going to get himself out of Rashid's line of fire. A quick scan revealed that Waheed possessed the only visible firearm. After pistol whipping me, Rashid had secreted his gun somewhere on his body. My path was clear. I took one deep breath and savored the complete calmness that had come over me.

The entire scene seemed to be playing in slow motion as I reached for the gun in Waheed's hand. I was not able to get the pistol out of his hand, but I was able to turn the barrel toward his head and with both our fingers inside the trigger guard I was able to exert just enough pressure.

Both sets of hands holding the gun recoiled but I didn't perceive the sound of a gunshot. The blood and brains splattering throughout the car's interior provided me with evidence of his gun's functionality. Waheed's dead hand fell away from the gun, and the recoil worked to my advantage as my hands were already moving in the direction of the next target. Rashid was sitting rigid behind the wheel. He had not moved a muscle as he stared at me through the rear-view mirror with wide eyes. This time the sound of the shot resonated throughout the car, along with more blood and brains.

It was over. For a moment I sat in the car with the deceased jihadists. The calm, serene feeling I enjoyed during the moment of crisis was now abandoning me. I began to uncontrollably shake as tears cascaded down my cheeks. Despite my diminished physical condition, I knew my job was only beginning. By this time, creepy Marwan was several stops into his trip to Manhattan. Waheed was lying with his upper torso inside the Toyota and his legs out of the open back door. I pushed the lifeless body out of the car and followed it onto the dirt road. My hands were free, but the ropes were still wrapped around my left wrist. I took a deep breath and began to run.

With only weeds and unpaved dirt road around me, I sprinted toward the only visible landmark – Shea Stadium. I was breathing heavily as I emerged from the weeds and onto 126th street. I tried flagging down a few passing vehicles, but no sane person was going to stop for the blood covered man with ropes hanging from his hand, running in the middle of the street.

The wrought iron gates at the prominently marked BULLPEN GATE were closed and locked. What really caught my eye, however, was the silhouette of a figure inside the gates. The security guard must have been scared out of his wits at the site of the male with blood all over his face, sprinting towards the gates. The guard had backed away from the gates and was on his portable radio screaming for help as I stood outside the gates pleading to use his phone. Maybe it was fear, maybe it was hearing me scream that I was a cop – maybe it was just wanting to make the bloody lunatic outside his gates go away. Whatever the reason, the seventy-year-old security guard cautiously walked forward and passed the receiver though the space between the iron rails of the gates. The old guard asked what number to call, and for some reason I balked at shouting, "911." Instead, I gave him a completely different number.

"Inspector Malloy, may I help you."

Everything became a blur from that moment forward – like a set of still photographs rapidly moving from one scene to the next. I recalled hearing the Inspector's voice on the phone and in the next scene I was lying on the cold concrete. I recall voices and people milling around me, and then the scene changed again. The cold, hard concrete was replaced by a soft mattress, and the people milling around me were wearing medical scrubs. As the haze in my brain lifted the reality set in that I was in a hospital bed.

"410" – that was the first thought to enter my brain. It was the room number I was focusing on above the brown, dull door. A nurse smiled kindly as she opened the door wider. Doctors and nurses surrounded my bed, working with IV's, a heart monitor and an oxygen tank. It suddenly occurred to me that they weren't attaching these devices to me – they were detaching them.

While the medical personnel worked, I tried to take in my surroundings, and an odd thought entered my mind. I immediately understood why people took flowers to hospital rooms. Despite medical science, there was something in our natures that required natural beauty as part of the healing process. We weren't robots, we weren't "units" to be fixed; I wasn't there for a quick oil and filter change. In their efforts not to offend they succeeded in not inspiring or lifting the spirit with the dull, clinical atmosphere.

I changed my focal point. An old TV set hung from the ceiling. A window that likely provided a view of the world below was just beneath the screen. In the other corner were two chairs, frayed with wear and tear. It was a typical hospital room, sparse and functional. Suddenly, one face dominated the space in front of my eyes. The young doctor smiled as he hovered over me.

"How am I?" I asked.

"I'll spare you all the medical mumbo jumbo and just say that my diagnosis is that you were pretty banged up – but nothing that won't heal with some rest."

"Do I have to stay in the hospital?" I asked.

The doctor shook his head. "No, we're ready to release you now, but I think there's a few other people that want to talk to you."

"How are you feeling, Jimmy Boy?"

I winced in pain as I turned my head too quickly toward the other side of the bed. "Inspector Malloy?"

Malloy placed his hand on my forearm. "Take it easy, Jim. You've been through an ordeal – just rest easy."

Memories were beginning to flood back into my brain. "That's right," I recalled. "I called you on the phone. What happened? Did they..."

"Don't worry, Jim," Malloy assured. "Everything worked out." He glanced over toward the window in the corner of the room. "We'll talk about it later."

I followed the line of sight and observed that the area under the TV by the window was no longer vacant. Three men in dark suits stood in the area. "Who are they?" I asked.

Malloy smiled. "Just rest for now."

I closed my eyes and sighed. "What time is it, Inspector?"

"Seven fifteen."

"In the morning?" I gasped.

"That's correct, Jim."

"Oh my God!" I wailed. "It's the next day. I have to call my parents and Kristin."

Malloy patted my shoulder. "Easy boy," he soothed. I've already talked to your mom and dad, and they told me they would call your girlfriend."

Before I could say anything else, one of the dark suits approached Inspector Malloy. "Have him ready to go in fifteen minutes."

"Go where?" I quipped.

"Trust me, Jim," Malloy replied. "This is not the time or place. Let's just concentrate on getting you dressed."

CHAPTER 14:

The clock on the wall told me it had been less than 24-hours since my life and death struggle in the weeds. I sat silently at a large conference table in the police commissioner's office with Inspector Malloy seated to my right. We weren't alone. Four NYPD emergency service unit cops and a sergeant sat across from us. I wondered if the Inspector and I shared their glazed, zombie like stares.

The conference room door opened, and the entourage entered, led by the Police Commissioner. I recognized the Chief of Department but did not recognize the other two gentlemen. The PC welcomed everyone and provided the introductions. Present along with the Chief of Department were Frank Sanders, Deputy Director of the FBI, and Ken Collins, from Washington. It struck me as odd that Collins was not identified by his agency.

The PC started the presentation. "You all went through a traumatic experience yesterday, so we won't keep you long." He placed both his palms on the table and leaned forward. "I just want all of you to know that your actions yesterday were in the finest tradition of the New York City Police Department." The PC seemed to be about to relinquish the floor, but suddenly caught himself. "And I'm sure Inspector Malloy would agree that Lieutenant Murphy's actions made the Sanitation Police Department proud."

Inspector Malloy nodded as the PC resumed introducing the next speaker. "Ken Collins has a few words for you."

The man from the unidentified agency replaced the PC at the head of the table. Even though I didn't know the agency, Collins looked like my vision of a Fed, with the short sandy hair and conservative dark business suit. Collins stood with his hands in his pants pockets as he got right to the point. "You seven hold a secret that must stay a secret."

The room remained silent as Collins continued. "You are the only people who know that there was a nuclear bomb in that subway car yesterday – and the secret is going to stay with you."

"Nuclear bomb?" I involuntarily blurted.

For an instant, Collins' expression remained like stone, but gradually, a slight smile appeared.

"That's right," he nodded. "Lieutenant Murphy was one of the main actors in this play, but he was out of commission before the last scene." Collins glanced toward the Police Commissioner and FBI Deputy Director. "I think we owe the Lieutenant and explanation. Afterall," he shrugged, "he's still going to sign the confidentiality agreement like everyone else. I believe Agent Sanders would be the best person to tell the story."

Frank Sanders cleared his throat. "Thank you, Mr. Collins. A little more than a year ago the Bureau began working a terrorist cell operating out of Saudi Arabia with Iranian ties. This cell appeared to be well organized and financed. Most troubling was what our intelligence source told us they had gotten their hands on." Sanders paused for a drink of water. "It has always been extremely unlikely that an entity other than a very few nation states would have the capability to build and deploy a 150-kiloton nuclear weapon. The much greater risk comes from the possibility of a much smaller weapon being smuggled into the country. It is well documented that both the United States and Soviet Union produced miniature, suitcase nuclear weapons weighing anywhere from 35-50 pounds and in the 3-5 kiloton range. The lightest nuclear warhead ever acknowledged to have been manufactured by the U.S. is the W54, which was used in both the Davy Crockett 120 mm recoilless rifle–launched warhead, and the backpack-carried version called the Mk-54 SADM, or Special Atomic Demolition Munition. The bare warhead package was an 11inches by 16 inches cylinder that weighed 51 pounds. It was, however, small enough to fit in a footlocker-sized container. While the explosive power of the W54—up to an equivalent of 6 kilotons—is not much by the normal standards of a nuclear weapon, their value lies in their ability to be easily smuggled across borders, transported by means widely available, and placed as close to the target as possible. Even a 1 kiloton nuclear weapon would be many times more powerful than even the largest truck bombs for purposes of destroying a single building or target." Sanders wiped his brow with a handkerchief. "The United States keeps very close track of these small nukes, but the Russians have never been very forthcoming regarding how they keep track of theirs. When someone with a good track record for intelligence tells us the cell may have acquired a suitcase nuke, we have to take the threat seriously. This cell was not only well organized and funded, but they were also tactically skilled. They assumed we were watching them, so they pulled a misdirection play. We tracked the mule with the bomb as he sailed from the Middle East to the Port of Baltimore in a freighter. When the ship arrived at Port Baltimore we were prepared, but all we found was a mule carrying a backpack filled with rocks. While we went for the feint, the real play was taking place to the south. The real mule landed in Guatemala weeks earlier and slowly made his way north with his backpack. He made it across the Mexican Border with a group of other illegals and was driven to Los Angeles, where he took the bus across the country to New York. The cell operatives in New York were two brothers, Waheed and Rashid Masoob. They were inserted into the United States three years ago and have been operating a variety store in Queens." Sanders looked directly at me and nodded. "All I can say is thank goodness the Masoob brothers kept a dirty sidewalk. When we found the backpack full of rocks in Baltimore, we panicked. We knew that decoy was sent for a reason, and that somewhere on the east coast a real operation was about to take place. Then, the NYPD received a call from Inspector Malloy, and all the pieces fell into place, but we had to act very quickly. The train the bomber was on was identified and stopped at Grand Central, the first stop in Manhattan. Lieutenant Murphy had provided an excellent description of the bomber and the fact that he held a pressure trigger in his hand."

I recoiled slightly in my chair. I couldn't remember anything about my call to Inspector Malloy, no less telling him that the bomb had a pressure trigger.

Agent Sanders continued. "We did not want a mass panic, so as quietly as possible the NYPD cleared the station. The only people we could not get out were those who were riding in the actual car with the bomber. The only other people still on the platform level of the station were the ESU officers and sergeant here this morning. One of the officers, I believe it was officer Peterson, quickly put a civilian jacket over his uniform."

All the ESU personnel nodded in agreement.

"Officer Peterson entered the car," Sanders said, "and when he passed the bomber, he leaped on him, grabbing his hand and keeping pressure on the pressure trigger. Immediately thereafter, two uniformed officers ran into the car and grabbed the backpack from between the bomber's legs. The sergeant and the other ESU officer then entered the car and terminated the event."

"Terminated?" I gulped.

"Yes," Sanders nodded. "While Officer Peterson and a second ESU officer kept pressure on the bomber's hand so that he could not release the pressure on the trigger, Sergeant Sweeney put a bullet in the bomber's head. The officers then carefully removed the bomber's hand from the trigger without releasing the pressure."

Agent Sanders turned to Mr. Collins and nodded.

"So, you see," Collins explained, "We had a happy ending. They planned for the conventional explosion to detonate the nuclear device, and they might have succeeded. The only casualty was the bomber, but the powers that be think it is a wise choice not to let the population not know there was a nuclear device ready to detonate in New York City."

I raised my hand like I was in school.

"Yes," Collins acknowledged.

"What about the bodies in Queens?" I asked.

"What bodies?" His response drew chuckles from the PC, Chief of Department and Frank Sanders.

Collins continued, "The commissioner has confidentiality agreements that each of you will sign. Let me be very clear gentlemen, failure to abide by these confidentiality agreements is a federal offense and you will be prosecuted to the fullest extent of the law."

I still didn't understand the secretive nature of this incident. "Why..."

Collins cut me off before I could get a second word out. "Let me repeat, Lieutenant, that it has been decided at the highest levels that it is in the best interests of the United States of America that the citizenry does not find out that there was a nuclear bomb in the New York City Subway." Without allowing any opportunity for a response, Mr. Collins was out of the door of the conference room."

The Police Commissioner became the main speaker. "I would just like to inform you men that you have all been awarded the department medal of honor." He turned to Inspector Malloy. "And I'm sure you will properly recognize Lieutenant Murphy."

"Yes, sir," Malloy nodded. "He will receive our department's medal of honor."

"Good," the commissioner replied. "And now for the bad news. You can hand them out now, Joe."

The Chief of Department placed confidentiality agreements in front of everyone at the table.

"Please read and sign the confidentiality agreements, gentlemen. As far as your medals go, the classified nature of this incident prohibits you from receiving the medals and you may not wear the breast bar on your uniform. An entry will be made in your personnel files that will reference a numbered police commissioner's confidential file. The only way that file will be released is under federal subpoena." The commissioner took a deep breath. "In other words, gentlemen, this incident never happened."

CHAPTER 15:

Present Day: I grabbed a Diet Coke from the refrigerator, but I couldn't move away to enjoy my cold beverage. My feet seemed to be glued to the floor and my eyes were frozen on a single focal point – the calendar on the refrigerator door. Reality had suddenly slapped me hard in the face. It had been 35-years since I joined the New York City Sanitation Department and now I was retiring. For all but a year of that time I had been with the Sanitation Police Department. As I stared at the calendar that had been provided as a giveaway at an Islanders hockey game, it gave me a moment to reflect. What had I accomplished during my long career? Had I seen it all; the good, the bad, the ugly, like my NYPD brethren I had originally yearned to be a part of? The cold reality was that I hadn't solved countless crimes, put the most dangerous criminals behind bars, or received numerous accolades for my service to the community. I laughed out loud when I considered that I was legally bound to keep secret the one big accomplishment I had on the job, which was a bigger feat than just about every cop in the city, or country for that matter. It didn't matter that I had risen to the rank of Inspector, to most people I was nothing more than a garbage cop. And why shouldn't I be? After all, even though I ran the day-to-day operations of the sanitation police, my civil service title was still sanitation man, and I would receive the pension of a sanman. I paused to correct myself. My title had not been sanitation man for years. My correct title in this enlightened politically correct age was sanitation worker.

I had been looking forward to retirement for the last few years. Patrick had graduated college and was on his own, and Kristen and I had plans to travel and spend time together. I also planned on spending a lot of time getting proficient in my new hobby – golf. But as my retirement date approached, I began to feel an overwhelming sense of sadness. The reality was that I loved my job, and I was having a tough time imaging life without it.

Earlier in the day I had left my office for the last time – that same tiny office where I first met with Inspector Malloy to talk about becoming a sanitation cop. The fact was that I had spent the better part of my life in that office and just like that – it was over.

The only thing left was the surprise party at Kate Cassidy's. Kristen and Patrick were horrible at keeping the affair a secret, but even though I was aware of the party, I didn't know exactly who was coming, and the fact that I knew about the party allowed me to arrange a surprise of my own.

I was happy that Kristen and Patrick had selected Saturday afternoon to decide it was important to go have lunch together at Kate's. I was no good handling late night events anymore. When I walked through the door, I made a lukewarm effort to feign surprise when I was met with cheers and applause from the guests. The dining room was decorated with balloons and streamers, and a large banner read "Congratulations Jimmy on your Retirement!".

As the party got underway, family, friends, and colleagues took turns sharing stories and anecdotes about our experiences. Some of my sanitation police buddies shared memories of cases we had worked on, while others spoke about the mentorship and guidance I had provided to younger officers.

As the reception line passed me by, it was time for me to experience several legitimate surprises. I had taken note of the wheelchair when I entered, but now I noticed that the frail-looking ancient man occupying the chair was being pushed by an aide and would soon be greeting me. I wasn't sure who this old man was, but I was going to treat him with empathy and respect, if only to recognize the unique challenges he faced in just getting to my party.

I hugged Jack Morrison, a lieutenant I had placed in charge of the illegal dumping squad five years ago. The wheelchair was getting closer as I hugged Larry and Billy. They had both retired from the NYPD at the rank of sergeant after twenty years and were now working on a second pension with the Transit Authority. My two buddies were replaced by the wheelchair. I leaned down and took hold of the bony hand. "Thanks so much for coming, sir," I greeted.

The voice did not fit the frail, shriveled old man. "I would not have missed this for the world, Jimmy Boy," the man declared.

There was a moment of confusion before a degree of awareness began to set in. "Inspector Malloy?" I whispered.

"What are you whispering for?" Malloy roared. "Who did you think it was?"

I was shocked. Malloy had retired almost thirty years earlier and I had lost touch with him. I just assumed he had passed away because at this point he had to be in his late 90s. "It's really great to see you, Inspector," I said.

Malloy waved his hand forward and addressed his aide. "Forward march, Debra. There are other people waiting to see the guest of honor." Malloy looked up at me and smiled. "I'll catch you later, Jimmy Boy."

I was quickly learning that friends you have not seen in a long time hold a special place in your heart and memories. They are people with whom you shared important experiences, formed deep connections, and made lasting bonds even if the experiences did not last for long periods of time. Despite the distance and time that had passed, the memories of my time together with some special people still evoked feelings of joy, nostalgia, and longing.

The hand I was shaking was evidence of these feelings for an old friend. "My God, Biju," I gushed. "It's fantastic to see you."

Biju Thomas shrugged and smiled. "I've been retired a long time and I had nothing better to do, so I figured I'd stop by."

I pulled Biju into a tight hug. "I'm glad you did, partner. I just wish Joe was here." The third member of my original sanitation crew, Joe Recupero, had passed away five years earlier."

"Joe is here in spirit," Biju proclaimed, "and he had a full life. Joe lived to have six great-grandchildren bouncing on his knee. Not many people can say that."

"You're right," I nodded, as Biju walked past, and the reception line continued.

"We figured we'd approach you as a group, Chiefy, so that you'd stand a better chance of remembering us."

There was something familiar about the voice, but I did not at all recognize the slim, distinguished gentleman standing in front of me who appeared to be a few years younger than me.

"He doesn't recognize us," chuckled the woman directly behind the distinguished gentleman.

"This is disappointing," announced a grinning man behind the woman.

"And I thought we made such a big impression on him," declared another man.

I began involuntarily stuttering when I had an idea who was standing in front of me. "Greg? You can't be Greg Wilson."

"In the flesh," Greg replied. "And it's a lot less flesh," he smiled.

"I can see that," I said as I eyed him from head to toe. "My God, you're thin."

"I made him lose the weight," the woman standing next to Greg said.

"Liz," I gushed. "You're Liz Hanson!"

"Liz Hanson-Wilson," she corrected.

I pointed at the couple. "You two are married?"

"That's right," Liz nodded. "After you teamed us up as partners in the IG's office, it turned out that we really were good partners."

I looked at the two smiling faces behind Liz and Greg. "Will and Walter – this is fantastic." I extended my arms to bring the four members of my IG's investigative squad into a group hug.

It turned out that the entire squad had done well for themselves. Besides becoming man and wife. Greg had bought a McDonald's franchise while Liz had worked for 25-year as an FBI special agent. Will had become a high-powered Manhattan criminal defense attorney, and Walter had decided to go to veterinarian school and was still a practicing veterinarian.

It was true. When you finally reunite with friends you have not seen in a long time, it is an emotional and meaningful experience. I was feeling a mix of excitement, nervousness, and anticipation as these people who had been so important to me passed by. The only problem was that in the forum of my retirement party there just wasn't going to be enough time to catch up on each other's lives, and to adequately share stories, and reminisce about the past.

My head was spinning from catching up will all my friends and acquaintances, but particularly, all those old friends whom I hadn't seen in many years. I had completely forgotten to keep track of the time, so it took me by surprise when my phone vibrated in my pocket. "I'll be outside in a minute," I said.

Before I did anything else I stopped by a table in the corner to check in with my dad. He was 88-years old, but still vibrant and in relatively good health. The old man didn't get out that often, so he was having a grand old time talking to some of his old friends and relatives, some of whom he hadn't seen in a long time.

I exited the pub and scanned the sidewalk in both directions. It did not take long to focus on my target. It was another man the same age as my dad who was equally as vibrant. I hugged this gentleman before taking him by the arm to lead him into the pub. It was time for my big surprise.

My old man and Uncle Nick hadn't talked to each other in years. The alienation became easy when Nick moved out of the neighborhood about twenty-five years ago to one of those new 55 and over communities in Suffolk County.

I led the man over to the table in the corner and placed my hand on my dad's shoulder. "There's someone I want you to meet. I think you know him." I said, trying to keep my voice light.

The old man broke away from his current conversation and turned to his right while extending his right hand in anticipation of a handshake. My father stared at Nick, surprised as hell to see him after all these years. "What are you doing here?" he asked, his voice cautious.

Nick shrugged. "I was invited," he replied hesitantly.

I was holding my breath waiting for the old man's response. I exhaled when he pointed to the empty chair next to him and said, "Well, don't just stand there – sit down."

It was far from conclusive, but I had a good feeling that I had brought these two old friends back together again while they still had some years left in them.

Even though the party had not been the intended surprise, I was still deeply touched by the outpouring of love and appreciation from my family, friends, and coworkers, and when it was time for me to address the audience, I took the opportunity to express my gratitude for the privilege of being associated with such an amazing group of people. I also shared some of my favorite memories from my career and thanked my family for their unwavering support throughout my time on the job.

I was presented with a plaque honoring my service to the department, and a cake featuring a police badge and the words "Happy Retirement Jimmy!" was brought out. With tears in my eyes, I thanked everyone for making the retirement party such a memorable and meaningful experience.

The pub became completely quiet as I made two cuts into the colorful cake. The silence was broken by a distinctive voice emanating from outside the dining room. Even though the dining room had been reserved for my party the bar was still open to the public, and this voice from the bar area repeated his call to make sure he had been heard. "It smells like garbage in the dining room," he laughed. "Does the garbage need to be taken out. Somebody should find a garbage cop."

Larry and Billy jumped in behind me. "It's him!" Larry sneered.

"What?" I was confused.

Billy clarified the situation. "Kevin – he's at the bar."

"I'm gonna toss that rat bastard to the curb," Larry said.

I grabbed Larry's forearm. "Don't"

I turned back the assembled guests, thanked them again, and told them to enjoy the cake.

"Wait a minute!" This roar did not come from the bar. It came from the frail man in the wheelchair. "I'm not going to sit here and listen to anyone try to make fun of Jim Murphy."

"It's alright, Inspector," I said.

Malloy shook his head. "No, it's not alright. I want these people to know exactly what this 'garbage cop' did for this city."

I knew exactly what the Inspector was about to do, so I rushed to the wheelchair and leaned in close to his ear. "Don't do it! You could go to jail."

"Jail?" Malloy yelled. "Let them put me in jail. The food is probably better than that place I'm in now." He wheeled himself back several feet to get a better look at the entire audience. "I want everyone to listen," he began. "Jim Murphy is a hero. Many years ago, he was responsible for stopping a terrorist cell that had brought a nuclear bomb into New York City."

There were audible gasps in the room. "That's right," Malloy nodded. "A lot of New Yorkers almost lost their lives that day, including Jimmy, but he was able to shoot and kill two of the mopes and call for help so that the NYPD could kill the third mope before the bomb could be detonated."

"Why haven't we ever heard about this?" one of my neighborhood friends asked.

"Because the government felt that people like you could not deal with knowing how close you came to being blown to smithereens," Malloy said. "Everyone involved – me, Jimmy and the NYPD cops – had to sign confidentiality agreements where we swore we would never reveal this secret, but I just wanted everyone to know that this garbage cop was awarded the medal of honor – but he can't talk about it, so I will."

"So, what will happen to you now?" Billy asked.

Malloy smiled and shrugged. "I guess they'll have to throw me in jail."

I wanted this to end, so I jumped into the conversation. "Inspector Malloy is a little excited, so why don't we give him a chance to mellow out a bit while we all enjoy our cake." I began walking toward the bar.

Kristin cut me off and grabbed me by the arm. "How could you have kept this from your wife all these years?" she whined.

I shook my head. "With the threat of jail hanging over my head, I didn't want to get you involved."

Kristin smiled. "When your dad called me all those years ago and told me you had been hit in the face by an opening door, I was shocked to see what a door could do to a person's face."

They say time heals all wounds, and whoever "they" are may be right. As I looked at Kevin I felt no animosity, only pity. We had been close friends since the first grade, and along with Larry and Billy we did everything together. There was a bond that seemed unbreakable between us.

But then Kevin, Larry and Billy went on the NYPD, leaving me with my poor vision behind. Larry and Billy still had time for me, but Kevin went out of his way to make me feel like an outsider who didn't belong with the crew anymore. Then Kevin got caught up in an internal affairs sting and testified against his narcotics team. He stayed out of jail, but he was fired from the NYPD and was labelled a rat. Kevin had become the outsider.

I had not seen or heard about Kevin since that time in the Swagman where he disappeared onto Woodhaven Boulevard before I even realized who the disheveled drunk was. And now, here he was at my retirement party, sitting at the bar alone, still making snide remarks. The many tough years of isolation, drinking, and trying to scratch out an existence were chiseled into Kevin's face. He appeared weather beaten.

We locked eyes as I approached the bar. I said nothing and moved in to give Kevin a hug. I sat on the stool next to him and we just looked at each other. I explained that I had to get back to the party, but said I wanted to get together soon. I could see that we both were trying to hide the emotions we were feeling. Kevin agreed to meet again soon, and we hugged again. Kevin got up to leave, and when we said goodbye, I felt the weight of the world lifted off my shoulders. I looked forward to the day when we could reminisce about all those good times during our childhood and teenage years. Would that day ever come? I didn't know.

As the party progressed, and I saw my dad and Uncle Nick laughing together at their table, I felt the weight of sadness lifting. I finally accepted that although I was retiring from the job I loved, I was not retiring from life. I still had my family and friends, and a whole world of new opportunities waiting for me. I could still make a difference in the world, just in a different way.

As the party wound down, I hugged everyone and thanked them for their support over the years. At last, I could feel a sense of closure. I had done my job, and I had done it well. Now, it was time for me to move on to the next chapter in my life, and I was ready for whatever came my way.

FROM THE AUTHOR

This book is a work of fiction, but the New York City Sanitation Police Department is real. The title of this book is my attempt at a catchy play on the link between garbage and sanitation law enforcement, but the members of the Sanitation Police Department are not "Garbage Cops." They have a long, proud history dating back many decades.

In July of 1936, in a move to revitalize the Sanitation Department and improve its efficiency and morale, Commissioner William F. Carey sent out 150 foremen and assistant foremen to enforce sanitation laws. These men, sworn as special patrolmen by the New York City Police Commissioner were the initial members of the Sanitation Police Department

They are a little-known force among the city's many law enforcement agencies: a group of armed officers whose focus is not drug dealers or murderers but the 30,000 tons of garbage that New Yorkers produce each day. But the importance of the work of the approximately 120-member Sanitation Police Department can at times be as important as any NYPD investigations. This fact came into sharp focus in 1996, when a sanitation worker was killed, and another was injured by a corrosive acid that had been improperly discarded. One of the main duties of the sanitation police is to see that such highly toxic wastes do not enter the city's waste stream, an awesome challenge given the amount of industrial refuse produced in the city each day.

In this case, members of the Sanitation Police Department worked closely with the New York Police Department and the Department of Environmental Protection to find the people who illegally left the deadly hydrofluoric acid on the street with regular garbage.

On March 15, 1994, two Sanitation Police Officers were first on the scene to aid NYPD Officer Sean McDonald, who was shot and killed while attempting to arrest two suspects for a robbery of a clothing store in the Bronx. The Sanitation officers desperately tried to save his life by performing CPR.

Even though the force can find itself involved in high-profile investigations, its other duties can be more mundane: making sure homeowners do not mingle their tuna cans with last night's leftovers, catching illegal dumpers and nabbing the dog owner who does not clean up after his pet.

The officers are trained much like other city police officers and told to always be on the lookout for confrontations that could suddenly turn violent. They undergo an eight-week training period, and bring to their law enforcement work a peculiar background: they all come from the ranks of the city's sanitation workers, having hauled trash or driven street sweepers. They can apply to the police force after two years on the job and must have a strong record as sanitation workers to be chosen.

Technically, even though their title is "Police Officer," sanitation cops are actually "Peace Officers," with much of the same authority as police officers, including the authority to make arrests, issue summonses, and carry firearms. Their more perilous duties involve having to stake out vacant lots to catch illegal dumpers or put on protective gear to investigate the criminal disposal of asbestos or toxic wastes.

The Sanitation Police wear the same uniforms and bulletproof vests and carry the same guns that New York police officers do. The only distinguishing feature is an arm patch that reads Sanitation Police. Their visibility as police officers requires that they sometimes respond to domestic disputes, shootings and stabbings, just like the officers of the NYPD.

Recruiters for Sanitation Police Officers look for personnel with good work records within the department and the right kind of personality who can use their heads when confronting a stressful situation. Once on the street, most sanitation police officers patrol alone. Most of their work involves tickets to store owners who have neglected to sweep their sidewalks or clean the gutters in front of their businesses, and tickets to homeowners and apartment building managers who are not recycling properly. But special units investigate illegal dumping and hazardous waste problems, like the dumping that killed the sanitation worker. there is also a canine patrol to enforce the pooper-scooper law.

In August 1981, in a move that was not popular with the members of the Sanitation Police, the department graduated its first class of nonuniformed enforcement agents. Sanitation Commissioner Norman Steisel said at the time that the new unit was better trained and more cost-effective than the sanitation police force. But after the first few years on the street, the agents, who earned significantly less than Sanitation Police officers, had prompted charges of a ticket quota system and selective enforcement of the city's health code. Some merchants and residents charged that the agents were concentrating on easily spotted minor infractions.

The enforcement agents are still in existence today, but so are the uniformed members of the Sanitation Police Department. While it was determined that the agents could take over much of the summons writing duties formerly performed by the police, it was deemed to be too dangerous for the enforcement agents, who are not sworn peace officers and do not carry firearms, to perform some of the more dangerous duties of the sanitation police, such as enforcing illegal dumping.

Most of the police officers in the Sanitation Police stay with the department for many years, but not everyone is happy. One former Sanitation cop said there were always openings in the Sanitation Police Department because no one wanted the job. He explained that the pay is the same as a sanitation worker, and working as a cop, there is much more work and responsibility to go along with much less opportunity for overtime.

I hope you enjoyed the book and this brief history of the Sanitation Police Department. On the following pages are some images of the Sanitation Police Department through the years.

Bob

Police Officer, Sergeant, and Lieutenant shields

Original Sanitation Police patch

Current patch

Original Enforcement Agent patch

SANITATION POLICE
Did you risk
a '25 fine today?
DONT LITTER

SANITATION POLICE
ANITATION POLICE

DSNY
POLICE

New Flying Squad roars into action. Anyone they catch making our city dirty will receive a summons for littering and must appear in court.

NEW YORK DECLARES WAR ON LITTERBUGS!

One out of 10 New Yorkers is still a litterbug. A new arm of the Sanitation Police has been set up to crack down on these remaining violators. It's called the **Flying Squad**. This 40-man patrol will blitz a different area of New York City every day. Every litterbug they spot will get a summons and must appear in court. Now read what you can do to help keep New York City clean—and avoid risking a $25 fine for littering.

Six years ago, a block by block survey of New York showed our city to be 50 percent clean. Last year, a similar survey showed our city to be 83.6 percent clean. The job of the new Flying Squad is to raise this percentage even more. Any day now, they will be handing out summonses in your neighborhood.

Read what you can do to help keep New York clean—and avoid risking a $25 fine.

Anyone caught littering will have to appear in court.

1. Use litter baskets. Put all light litter—candy wrappers, newspapers, cigarette packs, scrap paper—in the litter baskets. Do not use them for household refuse.

2. Put all garbage inside garbage cans. Don't leave loose rubbish on top of cans or on the sidewalk. Be sure garbage cans have tight-fitting covers. Tie excess rubbish securely, before putting it out for collection.

3. Keep sidewalks clean. Put all sweepings into garbage cans. Do not sweep dirt into the street. All homeowners and janitors are responsible for cleaning the sidewalks in front of their property.

4. Never put trash in vacant lots. Don't leave litter, rubbish or empty bottles in vacant lots. Owners or managers of vacant lots are responsible for their cleanliness.

5. Curb your dog. Walk your dog in the gutter—not on the sidewalk.

6. Don't obstruct sidewalks. Never put garbage cans or discarded objects where they will be in the way of pedestrians.

7. Keep containers inside. Containers for garbage, refuse and ashes should be kept inside or behind the building until time for collection. Then, place them on the sidewalk close to the building.

8. Have enough containers. Every building should have enough leakproof garbage cans for 48 hours' accumulation—to avoid overloading at any time.

9. Keep containers in good shape. All garbage cans that leak or permit litter to escape should be repaired or replaced.

Follow these nine tips and you'll be doing your part to make New York City cleaner than ever.

YOU HAVE BEEN WARNED 

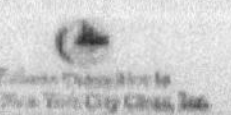

DID YOU RISK
A $25 FINE TODAY?
In one week, 2,792 New Yorkers received summonses
for littering by the Flying Squad of the Sanitation Police.
Avoid a summons—don't litter.

Did you risk
a '25 fine today?
DON'T LITTER

About the Author

Robert L. Bryan is a law enforcement and security professional. He served twenty years with the New York City Transit Police and the New York City Police Department, retiring at the rank of Captain. Presently, Mr. Bryan is the Chief Security Officer for a New York State government agency. He has a B.S in criminal justice from St. John's University and an M.S. in security management from John Jay College of Criminal Justice. Additionally, Mr. Bryan is an Adjunct Professor in the Homeland Security Department and the Security Systems and Law Enforcement Technology Department for two New York Metropolitan area colleges